CONTENTS

Writer's Biography

Adekunle is a UK trained Writer who has 24 Novel Credits to his name, 35% of the proceeds of this book will go to the less privileged villagers in Africa in which the target is to provide Clean and Edible water for more than 1000 households via solar powered Borehole water systems.

What A Coincidence!

by

Adekunle Adedokun
Genre- 16 SNL (Drama)

Main Characters

- Kelvin
- Emily
- Katy
- Mike
- Mrs. Madison

PROLOGUE

A pretty blonde lady in her late 20th was bullied and shoved into the shower hall by four of her fellow inmates all in the famous orange, the gang leader utters while she played with the terrified girl's barbie hair "pretty little thing, you gonna be a good girl for us right" she ripped off the shivering girl's orange top while the other gang members ripped of her trousers and black panties, the gang leader finishes the assault by viciously yanking off her black bra, her pointed nipple and C-cup firm breast bounces of the tore bra, her perfectly toned naked body with hips to die for- it amazes the gang leader and her friends who had more than few pounds in their bodies and bellies. Frightening and slurring her words, "Please I want no trouble please let me go" she replied "don't worry we'd let you go after we have a little fun with you" the other gang inmates fond with her breasts, bum and thighs. she cringes, The leader aggressively held blonde's hair in a full fist and pulled the girl's face towards her own enormous chest. she raised her own orange top and pulled down her blue bra revealing her Melon boobs " suck on it bitch" she obliged with little to no choice, The other gang joined in and she also sucked all their boobies, they shoved her back to the leader's boobs again, she shed tears as she reluctantly sucked on them, for the second time, the leader went on to say "Okay that's enough, now go down on your knees, it's time for you to go down low on all of us, a pity we are all haven't shaved that place for a while, we all doing life here, it's not like we going on a date with a man anytime soon, so we make do with what we got blonde" They mocked and taunted her, but the little girl has had enough, in swift second, She bit off the leader's nipple, She screamed in agony clutching onto her deformed breast, the other gang leader found their composure back from an audacious move by a girl they though so little of-they grabbed her and almost strangled her to death but in the nick of time, the female warders heard the agonizing scream of the gang leader and stormed into the shower hall, broke up the fight and ushered the injured to the medic ward and her friends into a cell hole devoid of light and space.

The warder got Blonde another orange cloth and took her into another hole cell similar to the other one accommodating the gangs. The warder spoke to her just before she locked the light off her sight "you just made the dumbest fucking mistake, you just bit off the nipple of THE kalifa, she the cartel leader of this prison, she controls half of the psychopaths in this place. you see this four square wall around you here ? is the safest place for you right now in this entire prison" The warder shut the door on her. Surrounded by total darkness, she could hear and feel her heartbeat racing in the dead silent little square room, she could barely stretch her legs as she reflect, the soreness of her own bruised cheeks and busted lips did add to her traumatized mind. For days she was there as she almost developed psychological problems until she heard another female cracked voice through the wall "Hey anyone there! The silence is driving me crazy here" - Apparently another Inmate involved in a gang fight had just been thrown in the hole cell beside her. The two inmate strikes needed conversation through the wall, she narrates her story filled with Love, Lust, Regret and Betrayal to her new colleague, she puzzled if her colleague will percieved her as the victim or the devil in the story she was narrating. Her name goes by EMILY and this is her story.

1 A BEAUTIFUL DAWN

In the Mountain Hills, as the Morning sunlight shines on the New York Mansion with breathtaking landscape, surrounded by Green lush Hills, The Mansion's beautiful garden was breathtaking as birds were chippings all around the palm trees, and underneath lied a thing of beauty, blue and white peafowls walked with their tail trains through a variety of colorful dwarf flowers and grass in the garden which faced an ocean view. It was perfect place to host the outdoor garden wedding of Mrs. Washington's son-Mike, the well-built caramel toned tall gentleman in red polo shirt and desert pants wrapped his hands around the delicate curvy waist of his cute blonde ex -model girlfriend who stretched to kiss him in her tank top and blue skin tight jeans- Emily. They cuddled up as they imagined walking down the aisle tomorrow morning, the groom's mother in her 60s dazzles in an expensive attire as she walked out to the garden, the wedding planner tried her best to get her attention, She gave up her attempt has the half cast mum stroked her natural brunette hair when she approached her son and his wife to be.

GROOM'S MOTHER
(Smiles)
Hey! Love birds, break it up,

MIKE
LOl, Heyyyy MUM,

EMILY
Hey Mrs. Madison, we checked up on you
earlier when we got here, but
Charles told us you are in the
library

MRS MADISON
Yes dear, was on the phone with
the Mayor, he said he won't stay
too long in the wedding, he has to
catch a flight to London

EMILY
Wow, The Mayor is coming!

MIKE
Don't worry dear, is just the two
of us that day.

Mike snugged his fiancée, as the wedding planner invaded their privacy again, "I am sorry ma'am, but I really need you for-" Mother of the groom cut her words "-Ok ok, you got my undivided attention Preciliar" she turned to the love birds "join us, we will try not to be too boring for you two" they all walk through the wedding venue.

The Washington's are a very wealthy and affluent family in New York City's Real Estate- Skyline Towers, Particularly what made them stand out was their charitable and philanthropic attributes to the correctional system- this was majorly managed by Mrs. Washington as she doubled as the COO of skyline. After the passing of Mr. Washington, their only son Mike, took over his father's position as the Chief Executive Officer.

Mrs. Washington became more vested in politics knowing fully well, she stood a better chance in changing the policies that was dear to her struggle for a prison reform – prison shouldn't be seen as a penitentiary hell-hole but correctional facilities which the inmates could be counsel, taught technical entrepreneurial skills and potentially make them self-productive to the society which wouldn't ordinarily offer them a second chance in job potentials.

In another continent where English was invented, the cousin of Mike who shared similar physical characteristics with him- Kelvin. He works in a decent box office in London-Blue Sea Agency', in the background of his office holding different box office workers in corporate suits doing their jobs, some looking enthusiastic while others looks like they came to work just to keep from getting fired.

After some minutes passed 12 o'clock noon, Kelvin was seated up at his desk, visibly tired and anxious to get out of the jam parked office building. His supervisor, A British old lady with a half frame glasses on her nose bridge, with a dress sense she thought was fashionable, she branched his office- poor lady, she has no idea she has being nicknamed Mrs. amoeba by her staffs

Mrs. Amoeba

Mr. Kelvin, I know you are aware
that you must finish your task before you leave your shift TODAY. I
don't fancy-

KELVIN

-Ma'am, please I have transferred
the work to Philip. I already told him about it, I
have a flight by-

BOSS Amoeba
-I don't care, please don't talk
over me. Now get that work done
by half 3 today.

She walked off authoritatively, yelling at other staffs to put
their backs into the work- A bit of an unnecessary behavior
to exert pressure on her subordinate,

Kelvin whispered to himself *"Fucking bitch"* but someone
over hears him-a geek with glasses thicker than binoculars.
He stretched on to the angry man's box office, while watching him from a dorsal view, he uttered "I heard that" Kelvin unaware someone was there looked up in utter fear and
shock!

KELVIN

Dam! o it's you Philips. My mind
went out of the window for a second

PHILIPS
LOl, yeah she can be a handful
sometimes mate. So what's that
about bruv?

KELVIN
You know I told you my cousin is getting

married tomorrow in NY

PHILIPS

Oh yes, better bring me some American cake, but
what's that has to do with Amoeba?

KELVIN

Yeah, so I booked my flight by 2
pm today, but that witch just
pinned me finish the Omega TV ad
today,

PHILIPS

That's terrible mate, what are
you going to do now,

KELVIN

PSHH

PHILIPS

Let's work together mate, I think
she went for her meeting. We can
do this by half 12 man in time for
you to catch your flight

KELVIN

Cheers man, you just uplifted my
spirit

PHILIPS

I   hate this job too mate but it
pays the bills

KELVIN

Fucking minimum wage

WASHINGTON'S MANSION

The proposed groom and his baby were leaving the mansion as they were joined by their friends in the parking

lot, which backed a magnificent water falls from mountain rock that surrounded the frontal part of the work of art Mansion. The groomsmen were trying all their best to grab dates with the bridesmaids- can't blame them; the girls have curves to die for. MIKE ran his fingers on the glowing face of his love, with a grin smile, he said "Baby, the next time I be seeing you will be in those beautiful wedding dress

> EMILY
> I still have Goosebumps, a few
> hours to my own wedding to the
> love of my life.

> MIKE
> Yeah am the lucky one baby, you know,

...as he stroked her Beautiful hair with both his hands

> EMILY
> Lol, now tell your friends to keep
> you safe in the bachelor parryy.

> MIKE
> You know I am a gentleman, and
> you should be safe too in yal'
> Party

> EMILY
> My friend and I just gonna stay in
> our hotel villa and take ice cream
> and gossip lol

> MIKE
> (Sarcastic smile)
> Yeah right.

They gave each other a goodbye kiss and both departed with their friends in different space wagon jeeps. Emily and her 9 bridal friends- 2 blacks and 7 whites, ride about the city having incredible fun from shopping to Cinema to spa, while they were in the spa, they sank their magnificent bodies into a wide Jacuzzi- the other ladies in the spa looked a little bit jealous of the girls squad with perfect toned bodies, lovely flat tummies and curves that matched the legendary music icon J.Lo, the ladies sure looked good in their bikinis all looking like victoria secret models. The ladies tried to outshine each other, some of the busty girls wore transparent bikinis which revealed their pitch perfect D-cup boobs. After their show of feminine oppression in the spa, The ladies proceeded to their hotel studio, she puts on her beautiful wedding gown and the bridal maids tried out their blue bridesmaid gowns too, The professional male photographer got invited for bridal train photo shoot, even though he's a professional, he couldn't help fantasize as the ladies changed their clothes right in front of him, one of them seemed to fancy him and gave him a little something to stare at, she intentionally had a nipple slip while wearing her gown, exposing her thick dark D-cup left nipple, she quickly covered it up, like she made an honest shy mistake. The man lost control with a visible hard on showing beneath his trousers, he tried to concentrate on the shutter of the camera but the firmness of the nipple he just witnessed got him tangled inside out. The ladies kind of mocked him after seeing the show of shame beneath his belt, one of the uptight friends of Emily voiced out to her girlfriends "oh my God ,Really, Really man, this dude is having a hard on, so unprofessional" He looks so embarrassed, he stared down as the girls mocked him.

LONDON HOUSTON AIRPORT

Meanwhile in London, Kelvin still in his office suit doesn't have time to change, he managed to catch his flight as he rushed through check-in line and securities, into the plane en route to New York City.

HOUSE POOL PARTY

Back in USA, A little while later in the evening, the bubbling house was lit up for the bachelor party as strippers in bikinis overflowed the party pool. Mike and his friends got wasted in expensive champagnes. Loud heavy music bars are audibly heard everywhere, as the strippers dance and strip their bikinis in the pool.

BRIDE HOTEL SUIT

Across the city, The soon to be bride and her girlfriends have all dressed up in different stylish and seductive short gowns ranging from white to blue to pink to maroon to black, but Emily dress was the best with a short skin tight red gown revealing her perfect legs and curves, she matched it with a diamond jewelries-Her friends knows Emily was head and shoulder above them in beauty and fashion.

BRIDE MAID 1

(TO EMILY)
Babes, Mike is a lucky guy, you
Looking hot girl!

BRIDE MAID 2
Am so jealous of you girl,
beautiful and marrying a
millionaire. hah, your life is a
dream girl lol

EMILY
Lol, common, stop flattering me,
let's get this party started girlfriends.

BRIDE MAID 3
Hey, club Guyana waits for no
one. let go, let go! the stripper
boys better be as hot as they say,

BRIDE MAID 4
Am just gonna get drunk as fuck, babes

BRIDE MAID 5
We know you and drinks, lol.

The other ladies joined in on the laughs, as they do final touches to their makeup in front of the wardrobe mirrors. The girls all in smiles set out to the hotel reception as other guests looked on at the perfect creatures dazzling in different shades of beauties; the bride diamond gifted to her by Mike outshines every other diamond in the reception by a distance. They are received by their Hispanic driver. The ladies set out into vehicle as they head to club

JFK AIRPORT

Kelvin had just passed customs in JFK international airport, he tried his cousin's number multiple times as he stared at different families and loved ones receiving their guests, some show excitement, some subtle and some utterly flat engagement with each other.

INTER-CUT SCENE BETWEEN KELVIN AND MIKE'S LOCATION

POOL SIDE

Mike's phone seemed to be ringing in the pool house room but Mike and his friends were carried away by loud music and the stripper's show.

JFK AIRPORT

"Come on Mike pick your phone "Kelvin goes on to send him a text, as he called for a cab ,He strikes needed conversation with the Indian looking driver

>   KELVIN
> Men, take me to the closest hotel
> to the city Centre.

>   CAB DRIVER
>   (Indian accent)
> Ok sir, guess you coming from Europe yeah, looking at your dress sense

>   KELVIN
> lol, yeah London,

>   CAB DRIVER
> Haaaa London, I have some
> families there

>   KELVIN
> Yeah, you guys are everywhere

>   CAB DRIVER
> Lol, you got that right, so you came to see your families too yeah?

>   KELVIN

Yeah men, my cousin is getting
married and his having   bachelor
party right now

CAB DRIVER
wow, party, no party like
bachelor's party man

KELVIN
Yeah yeah, But his ain't picking up
men, I was really looking forward
to the fucking party. You know to
blow some steam off,
I just don't know where they
finally chose for the party.

CAB DRIVER
I know the feeling boss man, I
just blow steam off with hookers
men. Straight up.

KELVIN
Lol. You crazy men

CAB DRIVER
Hey take their card men, you can
order for a girl with specific
styles and spec. I like and order   breasty
white girl ALOOOT

KELVIN
LOL, No men , you crazy men , breasty girls, that's
a new one.

CAB DRIVER
Come on take it, you know you
want to, men. lol

He stared at the card for a while but the lonely kelvin went on to collect the card as he highlighted and waved his new friend off.

CITY CENTRE HOTEL
The well dressed and handsome kelvin rolled his luggage into the hotel-though visibly tired and frustrated he was going to be spending a fortune on hotel bills rather than having a time of his life in a bachelor party.

HOTEL RECEPTION

> RECEPTIONIST
> Hello sir, welcome to Basbit
> hotel,

> KELVIN
> Yeah, Please give me a rather
> inexpensive room.

> RECEPTIONIST
> Unfortunately, we are fully booked
> for the weekend, However, we   had
> cancellation in one of our Suit rooms.
> but it just a little bit
> expensive, its $1000 a night

> KELVIN
> Oh! Oh my God, that's too much,
> ahhhhh, am checking out by half
> 6 or so. Is there any other hotel
> around here, I am from out of
> town.

> RECEPTIONIST
> Well sir, most hotel around here
> are fully booked too. This is the
> city Centre you know.

Kelvin was not looking happy one bit as stared at different rich couples who had no problem spending their fortune in the hotel, the receptionist tried to help him out

RECEPTIONIST
Ok sir, I can give you an in house discount of $250. Since you won't be staying that long as you claim.

KELVIN
Yes, Okay, thank you, here you go

The nice receptionist swiped his credit card in the POS.

CLUB GUYANA

In the late Night to Early Morning of the wedding, Emily and her girlfriends were having the time of their lives as they drank to stupor and cheered for the handsome coloured ripped men as they stripped with little to nothing left for imagination. Their driver soon came to pick them up in the club. He yelled at the top of his voice as the loud club song could possibly be heard by a deaf person.

WAGON JEEP DRIVER

TO

(EMILY)
Hey MA'AM you ready to go?

EMILY
What! Who are you?

All her friends were as wasted as the bride to be.

WAGON JEEP DRIVER
(Smiles)

I am the chauffeur, you told me to
come pick you all up by 2:30am

                    EMILY
Oh, the driver, you grown taller

                  BRIDE MAID 1
Nah, he looks Mexican, or Chinese lol.

                  BRIDE MAID 6
Nah, that doesn't make any sense he Indian for sure
right?!

                WAGON JEEP DRIVER
Please ladies, I need to get some
sleep and so do you all, the big
day is in few hours

                    EMILY
Ok Ok, girls I think we are really
tipsy now, let get out of here

The wasted girls staggered holding themselves as they
headed to the exit. The driver led them into their vehicle

BASBIT SUIT ROOM

Kelvin entered the beautiful expensive suit and went on to
use a hotel phone, he ordered for a bottle of CHAMPAGNE
from their bar. After which he received a call on his mobile
phone, The phone screen displayed Mike.

                    KELVIN
Really, now, the idiot calls me!

If only looks could kill. After he stared at the phone for some
seconds, he reluctantly picked the call.

INTER-CUT PHONE CALL SCENE BETWEEN MIKE AND KELVIN

POOL HOUSE

> MIKE
> Kelvin! I am soooo sorry men, I
> know I messed up, I couldn't hear
> the phone ring men

> KELVIN
> Get out of here men, you know I was
> looking forward to the party,

> MIKE
> I swear I'd make it up to you,
> where are you Please?

> KELVIN
> I Crashed in a hotel men around
> the city Centre,

> MIKE
> Please forgive me men, we are at
> Senator's Damon's house, you remember his son
> Chris, the wide mouth, he hosted the party, and it
> was a last minute location change, so we had the
> pool party here.

> KELVIN
> HA! I fucking hate you men; I just
> missed the party of the century.
> Chris's party is always wide as
> fuck, oh God, I hate you mike!

MIKE

LOl, I know you must be very
tired now, your tuxedo, is here
with us, we dressing up from here
to the wedding

KELVIN

OH, that designer suit cost a
fortune men, thanks for taking
care of the cost,

MIKE

No no, I owe you one cuz,
I am sorry again for the mess up

KELVIN

lol, it's okay men, send me the
address, before 6am I should be
with you guys,

MIKE

Oh fantastic men, I send the address in a moment, can't wait to
see you

KELVIN

Yeah me too, lol, men go get some
sleep, it's almost 3am. get your ass
to bed lol.

MIKE
(Smiles)
Oh mine that true, take care men

KELVIN

Yeah lol.

They both cut off the call. Mike was a straight up guy who made sure his friends didn't lure him to sleep with any of the strippers.

BACK TO KEVIN'S   HOTEL SUIT

Bored kelvin flipped off his jacket and the hooker's business card flicked out onto the bed. He looked at it for a moment and talked himself into calling the number.

INTER CUT PHONE CALL BETWEEN PIMP AND KELVIN

> KELVIN
Hello?

PIMP'S PARLOUR
> PIMP
Hello! Welcome to desires cuddle, where we serve you girls to your desired specifications.

> KELVIN
Oh, ok, am, yeah-

> PIMP
-Don't worry men, we have a lot that can tickle your desires, from Asian to African to European or Indian, we got some beautiful native girls too. Common men tell me your ideal fantasy. common

> KELVIN
Well, I really like white blonde model like girls,

                    PIMP

Now that's what i'm talking about.
We got one just for you men, now
what do you want her to wear?

                    KELVIN

Wow really?

                    PIMP

We are always improving in this
line of business men

                    KELVIN

Lol, yeah, my favorite colour is
red, I love short gowns with high
heels. it really turns me on and out

                    PIMP

Done! Where is your location,
men? your package is ready to be
delivered to you

                    KELVIN

Rasbit Hotel around city centre

                    PIMP

Say no more men, it's 10 minutes'
walk from our city centre office.
she be with you in 20 mins time
that I assure you sir,

And that will be $150, she will be
the person to receive the money
of course.

                    KELVIN

Oh OK, I am in suit 9 there. the
the receptionist will send her up.

PIMP
cool, she got it and she will be on
her way. Now tell the receptionist
she coming, I don't want my girls
being hassled

KELVIN
Oh okay men, sure,

KNOCK KNOCK !!!

He heard the knock on the door and thought to himself, that's too fast, I just dropped the call Now! But he was not far from the truth, it was his wine being delivered to him in a fancy silver container. After tipping the delivery boy, he patiently waited for his livestock package to arrive, visibly excited, he took the 'don't disturb sign' and hung it on his door knob outside. **BUT The 'Do not disturb' sign swigged towards the door frame and stopped the card door from closing-It in between the door and its frame**. Over excited kelvin was unaware his door was not closed, he took his hotel phone and made a call to the receptionist as he was going to use the toilet and have a shower afterwards.

RASBIT HOTEL APARTMENT

The 3 star hotel doesn't look bad at all, Emily and her friends tripped on each other as the kind chauffeur led them inside the hotel.

ELEVATOR

The girls and their chauffeur got an empty elevator, in which the nice man escorted them up to their elevator floor.

15th FLOOR

The elevator's door opened up, the tipsy ladies went on to their floor, however, when the chauffeur was returning back to ground floor, he saw a purse on the elevator's floor as the door was about closing on the 15th floor. He held onto the door and tried to get the attention of the ladies

> CHAUFFEUR
> Ladies! Please there is a red
> purse here

Emily and her crazy girlfriends turned back half way to the their suit number S8

> EMILY
> Oh that mines!

The drunken 'bride to be', moved in a snakelike manner toward the elevator, as her wasted friends went on towards the room without her; they held the card key door unlocked by using their high heel shoes to hold the door for her.

> BRIDE MAID 1
>
> (TO EMILY)
> Hey babe, we have held the door room
> for you!

Emily backing her friends just collected her purse from him. She answered her friends while backing them.

EMILY

(TO BRIDESMAIDS)
Okay bitches!

She turned and walloped towards suit 8, she was so drunk, she faced suit 9 instead, her eyes so dilated as she confused suit 8 to be suit 9. She goes on to open the door which was not properly closed because of the -do not disturb sign, this was coincidentally the room kelvin was logging; kelvin and Emily have never met before unfortunately.
While Emily was in the Suit 9, the room light had already been deemed by the occupant who was in the bathroom showering- Kelvin's room.

While Emily was looking around a bit confused, she heard the shower sound and thought to herself all her girlfriends left for the shower "Hey bitches, yall having a group shower without me. Bitches ain't loyal, lol" then the champagne in the fancy jar got her attention. She shouted "Champagne"!

The wasted lady popped the wine and downs half the bottle- like she hasn't had enough already. "Oh, I think I had little too much to drink now lol". She crashed on the bed and dosed off immediately

BATHROOM DOOR OPENED!

Kelvin walked out of the bathroom with the hotel's white rope, dabbing his face with the towel

SHOCKED!!

He saw the beautiful blonde Emily with short red seductive spaghetti gown with heels in his bed, her white seductive G-string panties were shown underneath her deep red gown which as pulled up a little, her laps was visibly so attractive, which make the man have instant erection, He stared on has he nibble on his lips-a rush of warm tingly sensation ran round his body making the room which was so chilled felt so warm all of a sudden. He thought to himself, can this be happening. He got back his tongue and mind.

                    KELVIN
                   (Shocked)
           How the hell did you get into
           here?!

The wasted girl looked up at kelvin in the low lit room who had the same body frame with her fiancé- Mike.

                    EMILY
           Hey baby, am I dreaming, come
           here baby

                    KELVIN
           Wow, so you just collect the card
           key from the receptionist just
           like that! that's just crazy!

                    EMILY
           Mikey stop talking, come to me
           baby

                    KELVIN
           You even have a pet name for
           me, your company is indeed in-
           novative, but getting the card
           keys from the receptionist, that's
           creepy but am gone forgive them
           cause you are so beautiful, so gor-
           geous, so perfect, I am loving this!
           All this for just $150.

                    EMILY

Come here baby, I want you inside me; I heard drunken sex is
orgasmic lol

The coincidence was unimaginable; the excited man thought Emily was the hooker he ordered. She was too drunk to think straight as she thought her fiancé was talking to her.

He grabbed on to the remote and played R'n'b play-list, coincidentally, the first song was R Kelly hit song titled "your body's calling" the light was already deemed, the mood was high and set, he glided into the bed like a pro Olympic swimmer, kissed her from her toes and worked his lips up to her inner spotless thighs, she cringed a little as she moaned louder and louder, he kissed her deeply there to intensify the sensation, she was smelling so good, he goes on to ran his chilled dark hands on her snow-white tights, he tickled her by making circular mild move a couple of times with his fingers on her inner right thigh close to her white panties, it sent Emily to a frenzy- she moaned louder now, she spread her hands in opposite directions and grabbed on to the bed sheet like her breath depended on it, her facial expression and her hair all tangled up on her face made her looked more gorgeous, he reaches on her shoulders and slides down the spaghetti hands of her gown which revealed her white rose push up bra, her pink nipples with tiny areola was already out of her bra from her constant turning- He gazed at the perfect perky nipples, his heart skipped a bit, He goes on to suck her left nipple passionately while he used his finger to tickle and nibble on the right nipple then he grabbed on the c-cup firm breast hard, she mourned and quivered uncontrollably, she held on to him now and squeezed him so tight, she ran her fingers tightly on his dark backside. This went on for a couple of seconds, he stared at her lips, she kissed him and he thought to himself *"I thought prostitutes don't kiss their client on the lips, Well this is America, I don't care at this moment, this girl is the most beautiful lady I have ever been with"*. The passionate kisses took up a notch, while her back was on the bed, she pinned him down with her legs wrapped on him all the while he buried his lower body between her thighs- showing the magnificent colour contracts of their bodies.

KELVIN
You are so beautiful.

EMILY
Huhhhh huhhh

KELVIN
...   I have to go get the condom
In the wallet, sweet stuff,

EMILy
No, don't, don't spoil the mood, come on

While her back was backing the bed, She slipped his manhood inside her as his penis brushed the tiny panties to the right side of the virginal wall, both can't hold on to their emotions. The melanin muscular man trusted inside of her and she grabbed on him with her mouth wide open, she breathed heavily as he thrust inside and out, she moaned with her eyes locked giving him her undivided attention while she held onto his cheeks. The seductive moan she was making made the sex even more glamorous to his hears, he let out he own too "oh mine, that my spot baby, that my spot, I am about to climax baby, oh baby, ooh baby"- his chest keeps beating faster than a sprinter, She voiced out "don't dear stop now"- Only Lord knows where she gets her energy from, she flipped him to the bed; she climbed him and rides him

KELVIN
You gonna use pills, yeah?
This is crazy,
I just came inside you! I couldn't
pull out which you riding me that
fast and wide !

EMILY
Humm humm

Both go at it again in the hot sex scene, she held on to his big broad chest like a bike handle, she goes on curl and twist while she rides the man, she bite her lips while moaning "Mikey! Mikey!! MIKEYYYYY!!!. She could feel him in her gut as her breast bounces, the bed shook to its core as she was about to climax, she winds her hair in all directions like a pop star as she worked a bum deeper into him.

HOTEL PHONE RINGS!

He ignored it of course, as they go all wide in bed, as they were about going to third round of sex; he placed his phone and the intercoms on flight mode- this is not the time to talk to anyone

EMILY
Oh baby, let make a sex tape, I
always wanted one

The drunken lady who doesn't know what she was doing or saying just made a terrible suggestion

KELVIN

Really, me too, lol, you are so
 different from others, this is the best day of my
life, this sex is crazy!
I have gone for too long, Oh I had missed home,
USA baby lol!

QUICK SCENE SWITCH!

HOTEL DESK

The call lady prostitute in a red short trashy gown, looking all uncultured was standing at the front desk of the hotel reception- this was the lady kelvin ordered for but seems he's got a classy and beautiful girl instead thanks to alcohol.

RECEPTIONIST
I am sorry; he is not picking up ma'am?

CALL LADY
That bastard, it was a prank call.

She placed a call to her boss about the situation, the pimp tried to reach the man who was having the time of his life-even if the president called him, he won't be picking that call. The pimp called her back and ordered her to another location- it was a Friday night, a lot of clients were on call in, She walked off unceremoniously towards the hotel exit.

BACK TO EMILY AND KELVIN

SUIT 9

The hot sex scene took up another gear, has kelvin videos themselves all through the sex with his phone camera. They both slept off afterwards. Few hours later, 6 am showed up on the digital wall clock screen,

Kelvin woke up first and went to shower but he paused as he was about to enter shower room, KELVIN talked to himself *"Dam. This bitch might steal all I got if I leave her alone"*.

He goes on to take all his possessions and slots 150 dollars into the girl's purse. He goes on to the toilet and locks himself and his possession inside. Soon after, Emily wakes up with a crazy hangover and headache, she looked around her clothe and pulled her gown down and moved her top and bra into position,

> EMILY
> What the heck, where is every-
> body, oh my head! Hey girls stop
> playing

...confused Emily looked around the room, with none of kelvin's possessions anywhere to be found. She goes on to open the toilet door but it's locked by Kelvin who just stopped his showers for a minute as he scrubbed his body behind the shower blinds- both didn't notice each other's presence at the moment. She grabbed her purse and wandered around to the door thinking her friends are all up to this- she didn't realize she just had unprotected sex few hours ago with a total stranger.

SHE OPENED THE DOOR!

She looked at suit 9, she thought her friends most have pranked her, she goes into suit 8 immediately as her room door was still being held by her girlfriends heels; all her wasted friends are still asleep as they exposed themselves

> EMILY
> dam! Were we that drunk! How

the hell did I end up in the opposite room, O God, hangover,
we must have paid for that room
too while we got back! I hope
I haven't mask out Mike's credit
card Lol, crazy night at the club

KNOCK KNOCK!!

The card door opened up as the heels were still held by
the door from jamming. The wedding planner, Pricilla
showed up in their room, she looked at the half naked
girls and she quickly closed the door properly-removing
the high heels.

PRICILLA
Emily, for goodness sake, it
6:20 am, We have been calling you
and the girls, your numbers seem to be dead!

EMILY
Oh my God 6:20!

PRICILLA

(SHE LOOKS AROUND)
I can see why you all didn't pick
up.

EMILY
Oh mine, oh mine, girls girls!
wake up!

The hangover ladies burst up, all looking at themselves.

EMILY (CONT'D)
6:20! girls, I am in trouble.

The crazy girls took their friends into shower room,

as they all stripped, tossing their undies all over the place, they showered together while teasing each other blossoms showing no respect for the time

PRICILLA
Girls rush up!you're playing too
much in there please. We are far
behind schedule. I am ordering
you all some coffee.

SUIT 9

Kelvin appeared from the bathroom all dressed up, he glanced at the bed

KELVIN
Dam, she's gone! Luckily I am
smart, she's probably pretending
she was asleep. Best spent dollars
on a hoe lol

HOTEL PARKING LOT

He proceeds out of the hotel, checks out and catches a cap to his cousin's location.
An hour later, the ladies also stormed out of the hotel and squeezed themselves in the wagon jeep.

SENATOR'S MANSION

Kelvin met up with his cousin and the groom's men as they embraced and dressed up in expensive wedding tuxedos. They soon set out in expensive vehicle convoys to the wedding venue

WEDDING PALACE

The girls finishes up their glamorous make up as they look

radiant in their wedding gown and bridesmaid's gowns, soon after, the bride's father ushered in his daughter, as the groom and groom's men all line up as they urgently waited for the bride and her father to walk down to the podium. The outdoor expensive tent was most beautiful as elite guests sat all looking glamorous. The beautiful bride walked hand in hand with her father as her gown flowed like an ostrich train behind her. Kelvin saw the bride from afar but didn't even recognize her because of the heavy makeup. In front of pastor, the couple read out their vows, Kelvin had a close up view of her and was getting the feeling like the girl as some resemblance with the prostitute he had sex with some couple of hours ago. *"Even her voice sounds the same"* the man wondered to himself. The couple kissed as they just pronounced them man and wife. Few hours later, at the wedding reception, the groom introduced his wife to his cousin.

MIKE

Babes, meet my cousin kelvin, he came all the way from London

EMILY

wow, thank you kelvin, how are you doing, hope you enjoying the party

KELVIN
(Skeptical)

Yes, it's beautiful wedding

MIKE

And will be a beautiful marriage

They all smiled and loved the humor, and then Mrs. Madison called the couple to come over and greet the Mayor as he's about leaving, kelvin now alone for a second, still as confused as ever, *"how the hell do they resemble that much"?*

he puzzled. As he was about opening the sex video on his phone, another white lady showed up from nowhere.

                    LADY
          Hi!

He quickly closed the video immediately and rolled his eyes towards the average height lady.

                    KELVIN
          Hello!

                    LADY
          Hi! Wow you are one of the groom's
          brother yeah?, you look so alike,
          maybe little more handsome and darker

                    KELVIN
          (Blushing)
          Lol, thank you, am his cousin,
          My name is kelvin

                    LADY
          Am I Katy, I work for the bride,

                    KELVIN
          Oh really, that's cool, I work in
          the ICT department for a marketing
          company in London

                    KATY
          Lovely

She kept staring at the handsome man like she was looking at the mirror

                    KELVIN
          Can I get you a glass of champagne?

OKATY
I will love that

Katy was a gold digger who thought to herself that kelvin was probably as rich as he looks. They hang out for a while exchanging numbers, kelvin then goes on to chat with his aunt, Mrs Madison again

KELVIN
HEY AUNT, the food is incredible

MRS MADISON
Hey kelvin, I know right, I literally hijacked the chef on her way to Milan for Vacation. lol

KELVIN
Wow, no one says no to my sweet sweet Aunt

MRS MADISON
Hahaha Yeah, listen, you must have heard that I will be contesting for senatorial seat yeah,

KELVIN
Really, no ma'am, wow

MRS MADISON
Yeah, Mike told me about your ICT expertise in London, we can use your skills in one of our campaign offices next month, are you interested? The pay is really good but pray we get in, if we lose, the job

becomes just temporal.

                    KELVIN
Oh my God, yes absolutely, yes
Aunt

                    MRS MADISON
Fantastic

Back to Katy and her friend Nadia, they both looked at the
direction of kelvin and his Aunt

                    NADIA
Cute guy, so you guys gonna get
down and dirty tonight

                    KATY
oh yes, I am locking that man
down, he is an ICT expert, I am
sure he's freaking loaded just like
MIKE.

                    NADIA
Emily hit a jackpot, she is
beautiful, has her a Millionaire
mogul husband, dam her life is
perfect

                    KATY
That bitch is not that pretty

                    NADIA
Oh yes, she is, you just jealous

                    KATY
Fuck you, fuck her, if I play my
cards right, I be out of that
bitch's shadow.

Katy looked on at the kelvins behind daydreaming. They

both were together throughout the wedding, they proceeded to the after party through the night, Katy has changed into a sleek grey long gown, and her heavy makeup did make her appear really beautiful while kelvin was still wearing his designer wedding suit.

Kelvin believed there was chemistry between them but little did he know, the girl was only a gold digger who needed some rich money bag man. Meanwhile, at the party, things got a little bit more interesting as katy and kelvin stole the show with their dirty wind dance together as Rihanna song titled "work" play on, this emotions overflowed into the private guest room in the mansion where kelvin would be spending the Night

MADISON'S MANSION'S GUEST ROOM

Katy gave the impression of being very forward toward Kelvin, as she didn't play the hard to get card. Immediately the door was closed She encouraged the sexual encounter with him by kissing him and grinding on him, she turned her back towards the horny man as she now faces the standing mirror attached to a dressing table, he unzipped her gown from her neck down to her lower back revealing her all net pink undies combo- as the gown falls and folds to the ground, right there he unbuckles her bra pin while at her back and he used both hands to held her boobs tightly, she moaned so seductively, as he slides his fingers on her harden nipple and robbed on them with his thumb and index fingers, she flipped her head back in ecstasy, as she kissed the talented man passionately ,she arc her back inwards which pushed her booty on him, she grinded her booty on him passionately , he yanked off her panties, bending her back, as her arms bends on the table, he trust in and out as the whole dressing table shake like an earthquake was hitting the house,

he pulled her hair back has he goes harder on the dog-
gie style. They soon concluded their sexcapades on the
bed and started some conversations.

> KATY
> HAA HAA, you are good in bed ,
> wow lol

> KELVIN
> LOl,

> KATY
> So tell me about your girlfriends

> KELVIN
> Lol, girlfriends? lol. No I don't
> have one

> KATY
> Yeah right dark, handsome and
> rich don't have a girlfriend.

> KELVIN
> lol, I don't know about rich, oh
> need to go wash off, come let go
> for the sex shower,
> kATY
> I will join you in a second.am still
> recovering from 10 minutes ago,

> KELVIN
> Oh really? we just getting
> started babe, lol

He kissed the babe and rolled into the mega bathroom. Katy
was still curious to know if kelvin does not really have a girlfriend. She grabbed his phone

> KATY

> Yeah let see your pictures, do I
> have a rival?

She flipped through the pictures in his phone and realized this guy was not rich at all, seeing his dead bit apartment, car and his box UK office

> KATY (CONT'D)
> Oh shit!, this guy is a broke ass. oh
> no, I fucked the wrong cousin, err-
> rrh, I should have known with the
> way he was pounding me, no rich
> dude has that kind of strength

She flipped to the video and saw the shocker of her life

> KATY
> Fucking broke ass liar, he even
> has a sex tape with his bitch, wait a fuckinh
> minute, this is Emily! this Emily !

SHOCKED!

As She saw Emily being rammed from the back by kelvin, she was shell shocked,

> KATY
> Emily! What the hell! boss Bitch
> having affair with Kelvin, this is incredible,

She checked the date and realized it was 4:00am today the sex video was made.

> KATY (CONT'D)
> No Way, no FUCKIN' WAY,   oh you
> are dead Emily, you are so dead.
> it's payback time bitch

(she pauses and zooms
the video)

He didn't even use protection,
am sure this bitch married Mike
for his money. oh am getting
some money from you Emily.

She goes on to transfer the video to her phone immediately;
she dresses up and leaves the room

SECONDS LATER...

Kelvin appeared from the bathroom all showered up, he
can't find his sex mate

KELVIN
Where the! Where is she?

(SHAKES HIS HEAD)
Girls here are sure crazy; they always leave without saying goodbye. Well guess she just needed a
one night stand. I ain't complain-
ing lol.

He gets some sleep, a few hours later, he dresses
up and gets ready for his flight back to the UK-
He needs to return to work because he's on night
shift the next day.

JFK AIRPORT

Kelvin was leaving back to London, he called his cousin.

PHONE CONVERSION

KELVIN
Hey Cuz, thank you so much
for the job recommendation, yeah
lol. Okay, yeah, I will be back by
27th.

Kelvin proceeded to the plane terminal

NEXT FEW WEEKS

Mike and Emily go on a dream honeymoon to Dubai, Maldives, and Japan, they return back after 1 month, Mike just bought a new mansion for his family and furnished his beautiful wife a new Range rover sport. All the while, Katy heard of all the great stuff happening to Emily while she worked hard in Emily's company with little to no credit from her boss. She can't wait to begin blackmailing the new bride. Emily soon returned back to work, as Mrs. Madison campaign started up.
Kelvin has quit his job and returned to New York to work for his Aunt and he was heading the campaign I.T Office of New York.

EMILY'S COMPANY

1 month later, the small glass house company which specialize in making lipsticks were doing relatively well in profit. The Creative Director just resumed work as all her female staff cheered and welcomed her back. Katy was one of the junior workers, who watched on in extreme envy.

EMILY

(TO THE STAFFS)
Thank you so much girls, you all

the best.

She walked and approached her conveniently among the staff

KATY

(TO EMILY)
I would like to talk to you in private

EMILY
Yeah one second but next time
use some courtesy and say please

Katy looks at her and gives her 'the oh no, you didn't' look.

STAFF
I saw Mrs Madison campaign ban-
ner today, I must say your mother
in law is getting younger every
day

EMILY

(TO WORKERS)
Lol, yes, now ladies, we are all voting for her, GIRL POWER! Girls, I
have another great news,..... I am
pregnant with
a set of Twins. lol

Cheers all over the place! Katy paused and added the puzzle together, KATY whispered to herself *"What if this bitch is actually carrying kelvin's babies, what if I wait close to her mother in law's election next year. Then go on to black mail her. I can scam her of so much more money like that. She'd do anything to keep the secret from destroying her marriage and Mrs. Madison's campaign"*.

She smiled as she thought about her blackmail plan.
As months went by, the campaign was hitting up. Mrs. Madi-

son had to relinquish all her chains of business across North America to Mike as she concentrated her energy on her campaign across the states.

MIKE AND EMILY'S HOME

Mike rolled his luggage through the sitting room, his heavily pregnant wife was not looking too happy.

> MIKE
> Baby, what's wrong?

> EMILY
> You are hardly at home, you were
> away for a month, and now you
> going again

> MIKE
> Things will get better my love,

> EMILY
> When? you are heading two
> companies at the same time, You
> know am pregnant and I need you here
> with me.

> MIKE
> I promise you, things will get
> better, After the opening of
> Chicago branch, things will
> descaled for me, and I be around
> your arms all day

The loving husband went on to kiss and cuddle his wife, then they went on to open the door in which a car was waiting to convey him to the airport. Mike goes on to close different successful deals in Chicago.
Meanwhile in the NY campaign office, Kelvin buried his head in work to ensure he does all he can to get Mrs. Madi-

son a victory.

Some months later, in Chicago, Emily goes on to stay with her busy husband in their second home there. She soon gave birth to her twins; Mike and his mum were in the labour room cheering on Emily for giving them two beautiful non identical twins. She stayed back in Chicago for 6 months for her maternity leave as she breastfeed her baby, after which She moved back to NY to resume her company work

2. THE IRREVERSIBLE REGRET

EMILY'S COMPANY

`Months later, she brought her adorable twins with her to work. The staffs are sure happy about the return of their boss; Emily goes on to greet her boss too,

EMILY'S OFFICE-DAY

>   KATY
>   Hello boss, nice to have you back
>   after so long

>   EMILY
>   Yeah, thank you Katy. but I wasn't
>   impressed about your report on
>   the Qudot company, you didn't do
>   any detailed research at all. kem-
>   bley had to redesign the project
>   again. Thank God we won the con-
>   tract

>   KATY
>   Kembley has made my life a living
>   hell in the office since you left. She

is acting like she owns me.

> EMILY
> You should sit up, I need all my
> workers to be in top shape. you
> got that?

> KATY
> I have a feeling you and I will
> become real close this couple of
> weeks.

> EMILY
> That's awkward, but am here to
> guide you.

Katy smiled to the babies as different thought went through her mind "*That left one right there definitely has kelvin's sleeping eyes. I am sure this is kelvin's babies, I need to be sure, I know what to do*"
While she stood there thinking to herself, Emily shouted at her.

> EMILY

Hey Please get back to work!

> KATY
> Sorry Emily.

She leaves her office, thinking on around her mini desk, after the closing hours in the office, she proceeds to her boyfriend's workplace.

HOSPITAL

Katy goes on to kiss her nurse boyfriend in the publicly owned NY Specialist hospital

KATY
Hey Zack, how my baby doing

ZACK
Wow, you never show up in my
work, thought you hate hospitals

KATY
Not today babe, you see I need
a favour but you don't ask questions, just do it

ZACK
What is in it for me lol

KATY
I give up my kitty for you,

ZACK
Really, lol you serious about
 that, you being in this celibacy
thing since we met ,you aren't
pulling my shit are you ?

KATY
Yeah babes.

ZACK
OK, Done, what is it

KATY
What can I use to secretly collect
blood samples of people without
them knowing? I wanna know if a
man is the biological father of his
twins

ZACK
(Shocked!)
What the heck, that -

KATY
- sh sh, zack I told you no
questions,

ZACK
OK babe, whatever, as far as I get
the kitty, there is a special tiny
tool we use for kids to collect
their blood without them even
knowing. It is almost like a mos-
quito bite, you take the blood
samples, label it and bring it back
to me. I will run some tests and get
the result for you.

KATY
Wow, baby I knew I can count on
you,

ZACK
Yeah come here, let me teach you
how it is done. We will use your
body as a sample lol.

They walked into another room.

EMILY'S COMPANY

The Next day, while still in the morning, Katy strategically
waited for her boss to arrive as she wore a ring which had a
tiny sharp spike underneath- The device would be used to
secretly collect blood samples without the host knowing.

Emily got to the car park with her husband who was doing the driving. Katy pretended as if she was just getting to work too. She rushes to greet her boss and Mike.

> KATY
> Hey boss, good morning

> EMILY
> Hi Katy,

> MIKE
> Hi

As the husband went on to carry one baby carriage containing the first twin and Emily carried the second twin. Katy quickly swigged towards Mike and helped him, thereby pinching him with the blood sample collector ring.
Mike felt the pain but made nothing of it, he kissed his wife goodbye while thanking Katy for her help in carrying one of the twin babies into the building.

EMILY'S OFFICE

Both Emily and Katy entered her office and set up the babies in their carriage, as the boss was lost in concentration with the other twin, the devilish skimmer used another ring to draw blood samples from the twin in her care.

BABY CRIED!

> KATY
> Oh baby, was wrong, you want to
> eat yeah, cutey cutey

> EMILY
> Bring my baby here please,

Katy goes on to give the baby to his mother, She used the third ring-blood sample collector in her finger to draw blood from the backhand of the unsuspecting Emily, her plan works, she had gotten three blood samples, she leaves the office immediately to the office toilet.

OFFICE TOILET

She bagged and labeled the samples,

> KATY
> 3 down and 1 to go. kelvin kelvin,
> I know I'd get you on Facebook. I
> don't care if I have to go to London
> to get my samples.

She looked at her Facebook messenger and chatted with kelvin who was her friend on Facebook

> KATY (CONT'D)
> Wow, he is online; I need to perfect
> a line

SHE SENT HIM A MESSAGE

> KATY
> Hey handsome!

But there was no reply, she went on to make up her face and hair, she returned to her desk.

OFFICE DESK

Shortly while working on some task Kelvin replied   her chat.

MESSENGER CHAT BETWEEN KATY AND KELVIN

> KELVIN
> Hi, runaway girl

                    KATY
Lol, how are you doing?

                   KELVIN
Am swell

                    KATY
Yeah, I am planning on going on
vacation to London; you know it
will be fun to hang out with you
there.

                   KELVIN
Lol, so you only need me when
you are craving sex yeah?

                    KATY
Come on kelvin, I am not good
with relationships, to make it up
to you I will take you out to lunch
when I get there, no strings attached.

                   KELVIN
Lol. Well I am now in New York, I
work for Mrs. Madison now

Her face lifted up in excitement, she can't believe her luck.

                    KATY
Wow, incredible, please let go out
today, the treat is on me, please
don't say no!

                   KELVIN
Okay okay, no qualms. I should
be out of work by 5ish.

> KATY
> Is a date, baby. lol

CHINESE RESTAURANT

They go on to eat and catch up on old times, the scene cut to kelvin's apartment as they go on to have sex again, she took the blood in the process of him unknowingly as he slept off, Like old times , she picked herself up and left the man in his deep sleep.

NEW YORK CAB

While in the cab, Katy placed a call to her nurse boyfriend; she planned to come deliver the remaining samples to him

> KATY
> Baby, you doing night shift today yeah?, fantastic , I am coming to you now, don't matter I will wait .

HOSPITAL

She handed over the test blood samples to him, as the boyfriend couldn't care less

> ZACK
> Babe, I thought the babies samples should be two?,

> KATY
> Eah, but I figured out that since they are twins, just getting one of them will give us the result.

                    ZACK
          Oh, you are right, okay watch me
          work baby.

her boyfriend goes on to conduct various test samples. He
brought the result to her some hours later.

                    ZACK
          Yeah, I got the result, so the man
          you denoted as kel is the father of
          the baby and EMI is the mother of
          the baby too. 'MIK' blood doesn't
          match at all

EXCLAMATION!!

                    KATY
          Please are you serious baby, you
          for real,

                    ZACK
          Hey this what I do, the result is
          right here in the computer, I will
          print it for you in a second.

She jumped and kissed Zack multiple times

                    ZACK (CONT'D)
          Baby, you gonna get me fired

                    KATY.
          Lol sorry baby, common print it
          out baby, lol.

Now she knows that kelvin was the father of the TWINS and
Katy now held the cards to completely destroy and black
mail Emily.

EMILY'S OFFICE

In the next business day, Katy was just arriving work at 11:am and walked towards Emily's office like she own the company, she busted in without knocking, sat down authoritatively, Emily looked at her like she was crazy

> EMILY
> Are you on drugs! You came to
> work at this time, called you, you
> refused to pick your dem phone,
> you came to my office without
> single courtesy.

> KATY
> What I am about to tell you will
> blow you out of your seat,
> literally blow you out, lol

> EMILY
> You know what, you are suspended
> for two weeks without pay. You
> need to reflect on your life
> decisions.

> KATY
> Lol, Bitch please, my decisions
> will be your priority henceforth.

Shocked, Emily picked up the phone and tried to call security.

> KATY (CONT'D)
> Let see whether you still want
> to remove me from this building
> when you see this video.

Katy plays the Video on her I pad and slides it towards her boss' side of the desk. Boss lady looked at the unfortunate sex tape featuring her and kelvin; it looked like a mirage to her

                    EMILY
What rubbish is this!, you made
fake sex tape of me, you superim-
posed my face in a sex tape. you
crazy! I get you arrested for this ,
you sick swine

                    KATY
        (point at the I pad)
        Shut the fuck up bitch, stop
playing dumb, that your engagement ring on your finger, your
freaking voice, your face, your
cloths, don't play dumb here.
                (MORE)

            KATY (CONT'D)
You fucked kelvin on your
bachelorette party, even without
protection bitch!

                    EMILY
Who is kelvin? I was with my
girls all through that day, you have
mental problems bitch

                    KATY
You are in denial, well let this
sink in, I own the cards to your
marriage and reputation now

Emily's face says it all, she is totally confused, the

video seems real but she can't recollect the episode.

She had a flashback on opening a door opposite her own room in the hotel

                    KATY (CONT'D)
          Wait for the big one now, I know
          your twins belong to kelvin!

                    EMILY
          Are you mad, don't you have ever
          talk about-

The blackmailer threw the DNA test onto the desk

                    KATY
          Open it, I took the liberty of
          secretly taking your blood sam-
          ples,Mike, Kelvin and one of your
          twins. Kelvin is the father. Just to
          make sure I told the nurse to do
          Mike and your own Blood group
          and genotype, since I
          assume you know them.
          You see it matches with that
          results!

                    EMILY
          What! You must be kidding and
          Who the hell is kelvin!? How the
          hell did you take our blood sam-
          ples, you're not making any sense
          , You fool!

                    KATY
          Oh please save me that bullshit, I
          am sure you being fucking Mike's

cousin for a long time, I took his own blood yesterday too, and with this result, I know his the father!

EMILY
You are delusional! I will have you arrested you bitch!

KATY
Nice try, well, now I am sure you want to keep your sham marriage alive, the secret will cost you. You married that money bag for the money, so I want some too.

EMILY was trying to pull her bluff, but it indicated that she was scared to death.

KATY (CONT'D)
I   want $250,000 by 7:00pm, bring the cash to me at the 402 Train station around the corner. If you fail to show up, you will become very popular tomorrow. Just imagine what this scandal will cost your mother in law's campaign, imagine Mike knows those twins are not his but his cousins', Imagine what will happen to your company's reputation. Imagine the whole world seeing your sex tape, imagine what people will say about you fucking your husband's cousin a day to your sham wedding, imagine Mike divorcing you. Just im-

agine. you losing everything

> **EMILY**
> Please let's talk about this, Oh my
> God, I was drunk that night with
> my bridesmaids, He must have
> taken advantage of me somehow
> some way. I don't, I can't remem-
> ber a thing, He must have raped
> me or drug me somehow, please -

Emily gazed   at the paper in front of her like her terrible life decisions was written on it

> **KATY**
> -See you at 7 and I was going to
> demand you give me a raise but
> I think I just travel far away to
> Paris and start a new life there.
> Well I got to go pack for the trip
> which you will be funding

> **EMILY**
> This is not happening; I was raped
> without knowing it. This can't be
> true, my babies belong to MIKE!

She looked on at the test result and she realized the result matches exactly to her and Mike's blood type and group. This has to be true. She broke down crying! She thought of calling her doctor, but surely this will be dangerous if the secret of paternity leaked.

APEX BANK

Emily met up with an account officer in her 'flashy office

> **ACCOUNT OFFICER**

Hey Madam Emily, How are you today?

EMILY
Hey Susy, please I like to
withdraw $250,000.

SUSY
Okay ma'am, you travelling or
something

EMILY
Nah, thinking of renovating my
office buildings

She brought in the bank POS, and does the necessary,
SUSY
Fantastic stuff, can I have your
card please

She was handed raw cash, she bagged it and left for home.

TRAIN STATION

At 7 o'clock in the evening, Emily met her blackmailer, in
the ever busy train station; they conversed in the loud environment

EMILY
I want all the tapes!

KATY
Sure, just give me the cash first,

EMILY
Listen to me, how they hell do I
know you won't publish this after
you get the money?

KATY
You just have to trust me Emily,

loll, you have to play by my
rules.

Katy handed over a flash drive to her.

> KATY (CONT'D)
> give me the money!

> EMILY
> This is crazy, I can't just hand
> 250k to you for a freaking flash
> drive

> KATY
> Your cash is for my silence, I have
> a flight to catch this evening. I will
> be out of your life permanently. I
> give you my word!

> `EMILY
> Please, just bury this, all of
> this.

She handed over the cash to her and she gave her another flash drive, Katy smiled as she checked the bag. she quickly walked to catch the next train on the platform as the door was about to close-seems Katy was very smart, she did that stunt to make sure no one can follow her, poor Emily just lost half of her fortune to a junior staff in her own very company.

EMILY'S HOME

In the evening, her husband just got back from a trip, she tried to act normal towards her hobby.

> MIKE
> Hey baby! Our kids are growing up
> really fast, I really feel guilty, am

travelling, it's driving me apart from my babies. They are friend-lier to our babysitters than me.

``EMILY
No baby, that not true

The mother brought her babies to him; they all played together, which portrayed a happy family. Emily tried to put the ordeal behind her as she went on to work. Meanwhile, Mrs. Madison was going shoulder to shoulder with her republican competitor, as she intensified her campaign. Kelvin was doing his part quite well in bringing enormous traffic through social media ads for his boss.

AMUSEMENT PARK

Few Months later, the young family were all having a great time during the summer time in the park, out of nowhere, Emily's worst fear came to pass as Katy showed up.

KATY
Hey Emily, How are you doing?

(LOOKS TO MIKE)
Hey Mike,

Emily was frozen as thousands of words ran through her mind

MIKE
Hey, we are great,

Katy went on to play with the twins in the cart..

KATY
They are growing up so fast,

MIKE
Oh yes the little two prince are ,
they sure are, LOL

Emily was trying to remove the stun look from her facial expression as she answers

EMILY
Katy what are you doing here?

KATY
Durrr, came to have good time
too lol

Mike looked at his wife like that *that is a rhet-
orical question'.*

MIKE
Who wants ice cream! lol

They all went to get themselves ice cream, Mike goes on
to pay, which gave Emily and Katy time to strike needed
conversation.

EMILY
What the hell are you doing here
Katy?!

KATY
loll, I followed you and your
hobby

EMILY
Katy please, please

KATY
Calm down, I am just here to say
hello and hmm-mm   I kinda need
more cash.

Mike walked up to the fake friends and they pretended they were having a decent conversation. Katy thanks Mike for the treat and she goes her way.

EMILY'S RESIDENCE

In the evening, Emily was visibly disturbed as her husband was working on his laptop while the babysitter took care of the babies.

TEXT MESSAGE!

She read the message from Katy- her face said it all, she was worried to the bone with the message; she wandered around to her room and came back to her husband.

> EMILY
> Babes, I be right back, I wanna get some female necessity from Asad stores

> MIKE
> Oh, but we were there earlier, you forgot about it that time

> EMILY
> Lol, yeah,

With a fake smile, She strolled casually towards the exit.

CHICKEN AND CHIPS SHOP

Emily stormed into the shop while the little blackmailer was finishing her snacks, she conversed with her in a subdued voice.

> EMILY
> How dare you summon me, 1 have

paid enough, you told me you will stay away, you give me your word.

KATY

Never believe a word of a blackmailer, besides do you know how hard it is to stay on budget in a 5 star holiday in PARIS. loll

EMILY

Listen to me-

KATY

-no you listen to me, I want $400,000,

EMILY

You must be mad

KATY

Yes I am mad, I am so mad that if you don't deliver my cash, I go on to blackmail your mother in law, am sure she has enough money to spear to keep this disgrace off her campaign white amour, but she would know everything about you, Kevin and kelvin's sons!.

EMILY
(classy eyes)
No you won't

KATY
You call me mad, yes I would, get me my money by Wednesday

EMILY

Please today is Sunday, I need
more time, please

KATY

Just ask it from Mike, do you need
my help as motivation

EMILY

Give me two week please, I beg
you.

KATY

Well, okay then, pay by Wednesday $400,000 OR $500,000 by
two weeks

EMILY

Ah!

KATY

We are done here, Good bye!

Katy walked out   on the terrified mother. The scene dissolved to the next morning

EMILY'S HOME

Mike in highly tailored suit kisses his wife and kids
goodbye and as he was about taking another trip again

MIKE

I will miss you baby

EMILY

Missing you already

MIKE

Mum's campaign is coming to
pivotal point, I am sorry I have
to go for a month

                EMILY
This is what we have been working on for the past year, go on
baby, we will be fine, stay as long
as you want. I love you baby

                MIKE
I love you too baby, am the
luckiest man alive, loll

They kissed again as his driver took him to the airport, She looked on as a mind was far from settled. The babysitter took the baby inside, as depressed Emily soon drove off for work on the ever busy Monday morning.

GAS STATION

She goes to refill gas in her Range Rover, then another regular car upfront pulls over by the gas station, it was kelvin in the car, he goes on to the shop to get some snacks. Emily's eyes popped wide open when he saw kelvin, she rushed after the man she thought raped her.

GAS STATION SHOP

She made sure he was standing along a shopping cart shelves, she launched a series of slaps at the man. People went on to restrain her as she shouted on kelvin.

                EMILY
You bastard, you turn my life into a living hell, you
beast!

                KELVIN
Oh my God, who are you? I have

seen you before somewhere

EMILY
Am Mike's wife, the lady youuuu-

Emily realized she had to watch her words in the public place. But Kelvin was so confused, the owner of the shop was about to call the police, Both Emily and Kelvin shouted at the shop rep together, "NO"!!!!

SHOP REP
Oh I see what's going on here, both
of you are in some sick relationship; Please don't pull this stunt
again here! Now get out of here

Emily and Kelvin steered at each other as they walk towards the petrol pumps

`KELVIN
I am so confused now; I have acted
like a gentleman even though you
assaulted me

EMILY
Assaulted you? You raped me a
few hours to my wedding; you
took advantage of a tipsy lady in
a hotel room and made amateur
video of it. You are a devil!

KELVIN
(Shocked)
Wait a minute, you the same
girl in that hotel room that day
right?

She slapped him again, bystanders take note again, kelvin was getting really furious

KELVIN
Stop slapping me, I have done
nothing wrong

EMILY
How do you live with yourself!

KELVIN
You are a bloody liar and a
pretender!

                    KELVIN (CONT'D)
I honestly thought you couldn't
be that girl that night, you freaking deserve an Oscar, You still
look at me right in the eye on
your wedding day and pretend
like we have never met. Why
were you for God sake still working a night to your wedding day?

                    EMILY
I should slap you again, what the
hell are you insinuating

                    KELVIN
You are the girl those hooker's
agent sent to my hotel room that
night, or early morning, You got into my room
with the card key I believe you
collected from the hotel receptionist.

                    EMILY
You are not making any sense,

                    KELVIN
That's the truth, I saw you in
my hotel room that very night,
meeting the same specification
of a hooker I ordered for, short
gown, white blonde-

                    EMILY
-What! You lodged in the same
hotel my girlfriends and I were
and you managed to kidnap and
raped me when you know we were
all wasted! You took advantage of
me, you Carlos bastard

KELVIN

I resent that, you called me pet
name called hmm mm, that name,
that name, oh yes, Mikey or something, you kept
repeating it

EMILY

Oh my God! How they hell did you
know that!

KELVIN

You were so turned on that night,
you demanded I shouldn't go
get the condom because it will
spoil the mood. Later on, you
asked me that we should make
a sex tape that you have always
thought about it but you were
too shy. I found it
really strange but you were so
beautiful I was not thinking
straight too.I ask you, you
gonna use a pill afterwards and
you shook your head almost in
agreement to me

EMILY

Oh my God, I remember leaving
one room. I walked to the other
room where my friends were. The
rooms were opposite each other

KELVIN

Oh mine, how did you get in?

EMILY
I should be asking you?

KELVIN
I noticed the door wasn't properly closed though when I was checking out from the room.
That why the pimp called me 8 times that night, the hoe never made it to me. Oh my GOD, what a coincidence!,

EMILY
A coincidence that has destroyed me!

KELVIN
Oh my God, Mike found out! I am so sorry, Wait a minute, oh no I'd lose my Job too; he got me this high paying job with his mother. I am so dead; I have nothing to fall back on.

EMILY
No he haven't found out but can I trust you, I mean really trust you about the words that will be coming out of my mouth

KELVIN
Yes I swear, Mike and Mrs. Madison have the power to destroy me from getting another good job here in US. They cannot find out about this

This scene dissolved into a classy restaurant with a lot of privacy sections

RESTAURANT

It was assumed Emily had revealed the whole truth to kelvin, they discussed on how to manage this potential problems which can escalade at any moment in time

>EMILY
>The last cash I gave to her almost ruined my company's finances. I don't even have half of the money she is demanding now

>KELVIN
>Can't believe that bitch could go on that far, bitch did a better investigation than the FBI. We have to be careful with her, she is very smart

>EMILY
>I am depressed, she is giving me nightmares, I hardly sleep at night. I am in so much emotional pains.

>KELVIN
>If this gets out, it's over for us but I know how a blackmailer thinks. She will always come back for more, she will never stop.

>EMILY
>(Panting)

What do we do?

                    KELVIN
                  (Whispers)
We have to kill her, which is the
only way to deal with an intelligent blackmailer.

EMILY really looked like she needed an alpha male to take
charge, but she was extremely scared but she knew this
would be the only way out now...

                    EMILY
Oh my God, like send a
professional assassin?

                    KELVIN
No, besides it is too dangerous,
Police go undercover a lot posing
as hired assassins.

                    EMILY
This look almost impossible

                    KELVIN
Like I told you, she is smart, very
smart, we know she must have
had copies of that sex tape, we
need to know everything about
her, if she has shared the tape with
others too, we will have to wipe
them out too

                    EMILY
This is getting crazy, how the
hell would we know who or where
she has transferred the tape to?

KELVIN
She would keep this a
secret, possibly to herself,
guessing how greedy she is, she
wouldn't want to shear the cash
with no one.

EMILY
These are all permutations; there
is no way to find out!

KELVIN
We will bug her home, her house
will be like big brother's house, we
will see and hear everything she
does.

EMILY
Wow, thank God I ran it to you
today, I feel so much better now,
just talking to you about this
mess makes me feel better.

KELVIN
Yeah, I have other tech to monitor
her voice over. We start tracking
her every move, starting from this
EVENING by 6pm, meet me at this
same point. I need to get to work
and get some gadgets in place.

EMILY
(Exhale)
Okay, okay
KELVIN
This was an unfortunate situation,
Mike must not know about this,

> I don't really care for my naked
> video being online but this job's
> 1 week salary is much more than
> what I earn for 8 months working
> in my formal shit job, No bitch gonna
> take that from me !

The scene dissolved towards the Evening.

EMILY'S HOUSE

The embattled mother kisses her kids goodbye as the babysitter sits with them as they watch cartoons. She leaves the house after a while to meet up with her new friend....

RESTAURANT

She parked a car close to the restaurant after she received a text from Kelvin which reads *'look to your left; come into the Black Mercedes heavily tinted van"*. She highlighted and goes on into the van,

HIGH TECH VAN

The inside of the van looked like I.T room equipped with state of the art tech technologies

> **EMILY**
> Wow, this looks like police high
> tech stuffs

> **KELVIN**
> Lol, yeah, Mrs. Madison did give
> me all the resources I need for her
> campaign. You won't believe the
> data I can monitor from here.

EMILY
Yeah, I can imagine

Kelvin collected her phone and installed some coders inside it

EMILY (CONT'D)
What are you doing with my phone

KELVIN
I am destroying the history
contact with Katy, whenever she
calls you now, it divert to this
phone I am holding here. Henceforth
you use this number to call her

EMILY
Why?

KELVIN
To delete any trace you were in
contact with her, when she dies,
police will search her phone
history

EMILY
(Worried)
What if there is a loose end, I can
implicate myself?

KELVIN
This is what I do, don't worry, we
will install a virus in her phone

EMILY
How are you gonna get her phone?

KELVIN
Watch me work,

> KELVIN (CONT'D)
> Now call Katy with this phone and
> stall her for some seconds, I need
> to trace her location.

> EMILY
> But I don't have anything to say
> to her,

> KELVIN
> Don't worry, just keep her talking

She goes on to call the blackmailer, who was living the life of glamour and riches

HAIR SALON

Katy was doing her hair in an expensive salon as her phone rang

PHONE CONVERSATION

> EMILY
> Hi it's Emily

> KATY
> Why are you using a new number
> to call me? you have my money!

> EMILY
> No, but I am really working on it,
> Please Katy, I know I can get the
> 400k to you next week,

> KATY
> Nah, we had a deal, am having my
> hair done now, so if that's all , I
> like to go please

                    EMILY
Please, no, just help me here. can
I pay 450k then, please Katy help
me out here, I am begging you here

                    KATY
Oh mine, you are really bugging
me, you know that? ahhhh, okay
because I am in a good mood. I
take 490k from you and it's not
negotiable. Now leave me the
fuck alone.

She hung up the phone on her.

BACK TO KELVIN AND EMILY

                    EMILY
Kelvin, you got it?

                    KELVIN
Yeah, good stalling technique

He goes on to do his I.T stuff which showed the precise
location of Katy.

Kelvin drove to the salon immediately, as they were
patiently waiting for her to step out of the shop.

                    KELVIN (CONT'D)
You see her?

                    EMILY
No. you sure, she is in there

                    KELVIN
Machine never lies, let just wait

Soon after, she stepped out and got into a car and drove off. They followed her discreetly, it now visibly dark,

>   KELVIN (CONT'D)
>   I told you she in there

>   EMILY
>   That bitch has changed her car,

>   KELVIN
>   She sure has good taste spending
>   your cash

>   EMILY
>   She will die with a sore taste in
>   her mouth.

Kelvin smiled as he tailed the blackmailer, she then stopped and proceeded into an apartment building. They pulled over not too far from her car too,

>   KELVIN
>   That must be her house

>   EMILY
>   Her car is more expensive than
>   that building

>   KELVIN
>   Yeah, let just wait a while here.

ZACK'S APARTMENT

Katy strolled in and unlocked the door; a loud sound of music could be heard from the apartment. She set into the apartment but its empty; she dropped her bag and proceeded to the bathroom

> EMILY
>
> Hey zack, where are you? sur-
> prise surprise, Just did my hair
> for you.

As she entered the bathroom, she witnessed the shocker which some girls often experienced, she saw her boyfriend sleeping with his colleague in the shower.

> EMILY
>
> You bastard, after all I have done
> for you!

> ZACK
>
> baby wait, it's not what it looks
> like-

She goes on to grab her bag from the bed as nude Zack holds on to her bag, trying to beg her. **He gave the lover boy a dirty slap, a flash drive inside the bag flipped out and fell into the side bed during the madness of snatching her bag from his grib.** She didn't notice, she grabbed hold of her bag and stormed out.

INSIDE THE BUS

Emily and kelvin sat as they perfect their plan, as kelvin was drawing out their strategic plan

SUDDENLY!

Katy stormed out crying a river and drove off

BACK INSIDE THE BUS

> EMILY
>
> I knew it, she went to see someone
> there

They followed her straight to her own apartment in a more Porsche environment

> KELVIN
> We have one week to carry out this research on her, every evening, we have to be here monitoring her, watching her, seeing everything she does, who she talks to, who she meets, who she sleeps with, everything. She will eventually reveal everything to us before we take her out.

> EMILY
> (Exhale)
> Okay

Emily tried to stay strong as she looked on at the alpha male sitting next to her. Kelvin wore all black, and he took out some high tech stuff. After 2 hours, as they were patiently waiting in the Bus, he set out his plan.

> EMILY (CONT'D)
> What are you doing?

> KELVIN
> We start now, I going out to tag her car

> EMILY
> Tag?

> KELVIN
> Oh I meant I am going to put a magnetic receptor under her car,

we will be able to trace her car's
every move

EMILY
Wow, you are so talented

He smiled and took a wine bottle as he left; the intelligent man averted all the street cameras and walked casually along the pedestrian path where Katy's car was parked. He dropped his wine intentionally beside the car's back tyre, in lightning pace he bends down, grabbed the wine and slapped the tracker underneath the vehicle and walked off causally, kelvin came back into the bus to join his partner in crime, he noticed the time was 11:30pm- *"it's almost midnight"* he thought to himself,

EMILY
That was so crazy

KELVIN
Lol, I know right,

He looked at one of the TVs in his bus, which showed a green dot and the exact location of where Emily's car was parked.

KELVIN (CONT'D)
Our work here is done, we bug
her apartment tomorrow

They drove off and they talked about their daredevil plan, she got back home and followed the same routine, her heart usually skipped a bit every time her phone rang because of Katy.

NEXT DAY MORNING

Inside the Bus, the duos dressed in black, as they watched and staked out the apartment of Katy,

> EMILY
> (Worried)
> We been here all morning, she is
> not going anywhere, she doesn't
> even have a freaking job, she
> probably watching movies.

> KELVIN
> Patience, patience, bugging her
> apartment will take patience. We
> need to know her daily   routine

As they waited, Emily's phone rang and she was growing frustrated.

> EMILY
> Oh my it my secretary, I just don't
> have that time,

> KELVIN
> What! You think I do? I abandoned Mrs Madison social media
> campaign ads to focus on planning
> and executing this problem in our
> hands, and you say you don't have
> time? really?

> EMILY
> am sorry, please forgive
> me, please

He fumes and focuses on his written plan as he studies his spreadsheet. Soon after, Emily set out of the apartment and drove off

> KELVIN
> I told you, patience is key, you

know the plan?

>   EMILY
> Yes, but what if the master keys
> don't work

>   KELVIN
> I got this from a very reliable
> car and a house thief. It should
> work, Let go,

The two wore rather large hats and funny shaded glasses as they pretended they were couples in love, and then they held themselves as they walked into the apartment.

APARTMENTS

They saw 6 apartments in there, luckily, there were a lot of bills on the floor of the entrance door, and they tracked her name with the room, which denoted her room number, then proceeded towards the door and they fall into their plan, they pretended they were kissing and caressing themselves close to the door, they totally removed suspicion as they keep up the act while grinding on each other, while kelvin used different master keys to try and open the door.

THE DOOR FINALLY POPPED OPEN

...kelvin placed a tiny 360 degree camera on the door facing the corridor. They patiently waited for the whole corridor to be empty, and then they set in.

KATY'S ROOM

Kelvin looked at his watch, which showed green dot light that was moving

>   KELVIN
> Katy is 3 km away from here; we
> have all the time in the world to

set out bugs.

EMILY
Where should we start?

There were a series of events, as kelvin orchestrated his plan, his assistance helped as they planted a hidden video camera and microphone in every room inside the apartment including the shower.

EMILY
What if someone sees us, when
we open the front door?

KELVIN
You surprise me, you weren't
paying attention when I slap a
tiny 360 camera on the door. I
have been watching the corridor
ever since we are in this room

EMILY
You are incredible, you know that
right?

He looked at his other I pad and viewed the corridor, everything looked clear,

KELVIN
Yeah, let's get out of here, we are
clear to go.

They set out of the building back to their bus at the next street.

INSIDE THE BUS

Kelvin goes on to open some drinks from the bus fridge

for themselves for a job well done.

> KELVIN
>
> We now have to bug her phone,
> which will be extremely difficult

> EMILY
>
> Is the house bug not enough, that
> looks impossible

> KELVIN
>
> Nah, we need to hear all of her
> conversations, she might have
> given the tape to her associate
> for safekeeping.

> KELVIN (CONT'D)
>
> Well, Katy is 16 km away from
> here, so it would be pointless to
> stay here. let go get some work
> done, but we reconvene by 6 hundred hours.

> EMILY
>
> Yeah, OK captain,

They drove along to where she was packed.

Series of events played on, as Emily and Kelvin went on about their workplace activities, the scene closed with both of them meeting up later.

KATY'S NEIGHBOURHOOD

BACK TO EMILY AND KELVIN

They both sat and had Chinese noodles as they waited for Katy.

                    KELVIN
              She is a km away now

                    EMILY
                  (Exhales)
              Am so scared, this is such a
              daring plan

                    KELVIN
              It will work, here take this, I
              will hear every word you say,

BACK TO KATY

She looked tired as she highlighted from her car to
her apartment

BACK TO KATY AND KELVIN

They are watching Katy as she moves in the corridor to her
apartment,

She set into her apartment and went to get a drink and
went to take a shower but left HER PHONE IN THE BED.
Kelvin prepared to go into her room and bug the phone
while she was showering.

                    KELVIN
              Yeah, Guide me into her room.
              Your code name is pepperoni and
              mine is Onions,

                    EMILY
              Okay, let do this

Kelvin wore another disguise as he dresses up like a delivery pizza man; he goes on to the building

CORRIDOR

Visibly dark outside, the street light were out, Kelvin walked via different people minding their own business, he speaks to his accomplice via his ear piece,

INTER SCENE CONVERSATION   BETWEEN EMILY AND KELVIN VIA EARPIECE

          KELVIN
Pepperoni?

          EMILY
Onions

          KELVIN
What is she doing now?

          EMILY
Undressing, she about to enter
the shower

          KELVIN
Fantastic, her phone is still in
her bed yeah?

          EMILY
Affirmative

          KELVIN
You are a natural with this. watch
my back from outside, the corridor is clear

          EMILY
The entrance is clear too, go
agent pepperoni

Kelvin smiled as he went into the apartment, he tiptoed into her bed side, as Emily was watching Katy over the TV in the bus. Kelvin unscrewed the phone and inserted a microchip inside.

Emily sees another delivering guy entering the building but she focuses her attention on Katy. Suddenly, the guy banged on the door of Katy and called her phone immediately. Kelvin paused as he heard the knock,

EMILY

Kelvin, sorry pepperoni, someone
is at the door, someone is at the door ,a delivering
guy

… The phone goes on to ring as kelvin was assembling back the phone

BACK TO KATY

She switches her shower off immediately and plans to rush to get the phone

BACK TO THE CONVERSATION BETWEEN
KELVIN AND EMILY

EMILY

Please hide, she is coming out! I
think that guy at the door is calling her,

NICK OF TIME!

Kelvin quickly slide under the bed as Katy almost saw him, she goes on to pick the phone

PHONE CONVERSATION

KATY

Hey! Oh you here, sorry I was in
the shower, one second please, I
BE RIGHT THERE

The strange thing was that the cover case of the phone was
not on the bed and she knew her phone case can't just walk
away,

                    KATY (CONT'D)
How the hell did this case flip
out,

She goes in a towel and get her purse as she meet up with
The Arab delivering guy

OPEN DOORS!

                    DELIVERING GUY
Ma'am, here you go

                    KATY
Hey   thank you. You so cute, what
your name

                    DELIVERING GUY
Zanzibar

                    KATY
Love the way you pronounce it

                    ZANZIBAR
Lol, thank you, here you go

                    KATY
Hope you put the extra source I requested ?

                    ZANZIBAR
Absolutely

Katy goes on to write her number on the $100 note she handed over to him

> ZANZIBAR (CONT'D)
> Sorry ma'am can you break it a
> little bit, I don't have the
> change

> KATY
> Keep the change and the number lol

> ZANZIBAR
> Lol, thanks ma'am

> KATY
> You better drop the formal
> attitude and call me.

He nodded as he walked away, Katy kept looking at his ass, she then closed the door and went to her bedside, Meanwhile, kelvin was still under the bed; Katy went on to remove the wrap of her food but the tiny source container fell down and rolled under the bed...

KELVIN EYES POPS WIDE OPEN

Emily knew she had to save her partner or all was lost, if he was made. Katy squatted to get the container from under the bed, as her eyes were about viewing the under bed, her phone rang!!!!!

NICK OF TIME!

It was Emily that called Katy, the call came in just right about Katy was about looking under the bed to retrieve her source package, she rose up and checked the phone. "you better have my money bitch"

PHONE CONVERSATION BETWEEN KATY AND EMILY

> KATY
>
> Yeah

> EMILY
>
> Katy, just want to tell you I am
> doing all I can to get the money
> and I have raised some now, you
> get your money, please don't
> expose me

Kelvin quickly slides the source out, towards the bed beside

> KATY
>
> Yeah yeah, you becoming annoying
> this days, jeez, just get the
> money to me by deadline

She cut off the phone and strange enough she looked down and saw her tomato source was there. She was shocked, but smiled and grabbed it as she ate away. 2 hours later, the scene dissolved to Katy in her sitting room as she was enjoying her show, then she began to have some rumble in her tummy.

> KATY (CONT'D)
>
> Whuuuu, I knew   I heard too much
> of the chicken.

She rushes into the toilet; this gives kelvin a chance to get out!

CONVERSATION BETWEEN EMILY AND KELVIN

> EMILY
>
> Get out now! The corridor and
> the entrances are clear!

He tiptoe out of the apartment and moved with pace out of the building back to the bus

INSIDE THE BUS

> KELVIN
> Shit! I thought I would sleep in
> that   bitch's under bed.

> EMILY
> That was some crazy stuff,

> KELVIN
> No shit lol

They kind of find the whole roller coaster mission amusing and intriguing. They drove off to their homes to call it a night. In a series of event as they [Emily and kelvin] watched her every move, sometimes together, few time at their individual work place, they monitored who she talks to, day in, day out, every day, they discovered where she hid all her priced possessions in her hidden safe box in which, they now have the combination to the save by watching her, she keeps two flash drives containing the sex tapes, and cash in it too, she checks her laptop and phone occasionally to view the sex tape-her money maker. The Pizza boy came back and hooked up with Katy in her apartment as they went at it. They engaged in hot sex, Emily and kelvin watches it like it Big brother show.

INSIDE THE BUS

4 days later, at about 12am at night, Kelvin did a detailed writing on the spreadsheet, showing the schedule and routine of Katy.

> KELVIN
> Time of truth, we have dis-

covered all we need to know
about her now

EMILY
I am so scared, but I know this is
the only way, she will surely cause
me problems tomorrow, my deadline is tomorrow

KELVIN
Her deadline is today! you know
the plan, let go

Emily and Kelvin held hands as they entered the apartment, the corridor was clear, which made their mission
easier. They proceeded in and viewed Katy from there I
pad camera. They sneaked into her apartment as she was
already fast asleep in the dream world- a dream which
would soon become a nightmare which she might never
wake up from. The amateur assassin duo covered all
their prints, they began crawling on the floor towards the
bedroom, they opened the bedroom door discreetly and
viewed her reaction from their I pad but she was still deep
in sleep, They crawled to her bedside, he gave his accomplice the signal.

SUFFOCATE!

In a rehearsed plan, Kelvin placed a pillow on her nose and
held her arms while Emily pinned down her legs, she busted
up from sleep all disoriented but it was too little too late
for her now. Shortly later, she pretended that she was dead
but kelvin was too clinical to believe that trick, he looks at
his time and still held onto the pillow. She burst to life again
which caught Emily by surprise but not Kelvin – the heart-
less man showed no fear or remorse, almost felt like he was
a professional assassin. She dies soon enough, kelvin made

sure of it. Emily was shaking, the alpha male held her and gave her the "keep your shit together look" -they made it look like an accident.

Kelvin goes on to remove all the secret cameras and audios from the room, he opened the safe and deleted all the flash drive content, laptop's content, also i-cloud and phone contents, he replaced the contents with porn videos and other non-essentials virus. They return everything back to the way it was earlier,

Emily leaves first as kelvin reap off the hidden camera on the corridor walls. They are clinical as they made sure no one saw them as they went out of the building.

They walked hand in hand towards the car, Emily dropped her purse near Katy's tyre, and he quickly grabbed her bag and the tracker underneath Katy's vehicle. The fake couple proceeded towards their bus strategically averting the entire street camera.

INSIDE THE BUS

Emotional Emily was shaking uncontrollably as Kelvin was trying to be a man; he held on to Emily, she began to cry like a baby. Kelvin now held on tightly to her, in this moment of weakness, they both stared into each other eyes for a couple of seconds which felt like an eternity of chemistry between the duos. Kelvin kissed him and they both go at it like they have been starved of sex for years. He stripped of her pink top which revealed her pink bra, he lifted the bra a little bit up, as he took a sneak peak at the nipple underneath as it bounced out from the fabric, he went all out and sucked on the perfect perky nipple, she moaned, her voice which was filled with stress a second ago, now suddenly sound so sweet and glamorous. He sat down on the 360 chair and drew her close as she stood in front of him, he took off her jeans and panties, she sat on him as they faces each other, they kissed for a second, she grinds on him back to front like rocking boat for a while, as she was now so wet, she goes on to bounce on him, her breast bounced along the face of kelvin, he takes over responsibility and while her body was on him, her hands wrapped against his broad shoulders, he stood up still holding on to her bum, He long broad penis was still inside her and he fucked her without care right there in the tech bus, she loved this alpha male sex style-as the bus was shaking like it ran into a pot hole, they go at it like porn stars.

3. THE BETRAYAL

Soon after the hot spicy sex, they laid on themselves and they engaged with each after the show of infidelity.

EMILY
I have never felt like that before

KELVIN
What do you mean

`EMILY
I mean I have never had an orgasm, until this very Night. I thought it was just a myth

KELVIN
Get out of here, you lying

EMILY
I swear, I have only been with two men in my life , the first guy was a gig, he didn't know what he was doing, then here comes Mike, he suffers from erectile dysfunction, he tries blue pill but his condition seems to be very acute, 2 mins at

it, his already out cold.

KELVIN
Wow, you don't say

EMILY
I mean this week we did crazy things that blew my boring routine life out of the water, you being the alpha male just got me all excited as you took charge. I love it when a man takes charge

KELVIN
I must say Emily, everyday I saw you, I Imagine tearing off your cloth and giving you the truth, but I had to remain focused, but it wasn't easy, you are really, really beautiful.

EMILY
Hunnnnn, come here pepperoni

They kiss through the night away like there were in a relationship.

EMILY'S OFFICE

In the next day, the rejuvenated Boss glowed as she returned to work fully doing her thing with her workers. Soon after she start to remember her hot steamy orgasmic sex with kelvin, she bite her lips and closes her eyes, she can't get over the dude as she was lost in imaginations.

The affair soon became more of a relationship as they had sex in different places in different days as Emily and kelvin were having sex in the bus, in kelvin's apartments, they can't get hold of themselves. They seem to love each other now and the sex was amazing- what a good sex can do to a faithful married woman. Kelvin was extremely creative with his fore play, every sex section was mystery accompanied by wonderful sexcapades.

Two days later, Emily was playing with her kids, but she was almost obsessed with kelvin at this moment. She called the babysitter who was just resuming her Night shift

> EMILY
> Hey, Listen, I think I can take care of the kids at Night and henceforth, they are grown enough now,

> BABYSITTER
> Ma'am but I am only need the money, please, I can do morning while the other babysitter do afternoon and evening

> EMILY
> Yeah, but that will be a waste of money, the other babysitter handles the job well during her shift. But come over to my office tomorrow and we can get you a job there, nothing to fancy but you get by.

> BABYSITTER
> Bless you Ma'am

The babysitter goes her way; Emily goes on to tug her babies to sleep. She went on to call her the lover boy.

EMILY PORSCHE MANSION

Late in the Evening, Soon enough Kelvin arrived and

strolled towards the back gate of their mansion, she let himself in with the automatic control door. They go at it again like they are sex addicts, grinding and screaming in her matrimonial bed, he spilled ice cream on her nipple, neck and thighs as he licked it all off her, she rolled eye towards her hair as she moaned, heavy breathing as she moaned louder. Soon enough, they went to shower, while in there as they bath covered in soap, he turned her back to him, and he rammed her from the back as the shower falls on them, he pinned her against the tiles as they took the sex up a notch, they finished up their adulterous act and they proceeded to the children room

TWINS ROOM

Kelvin was a little bit emotional as he saw the beautiful twins sleeping like angels.

> KELVIN'
> They are adorable

> EMILY
> Yes they are, he has your eyes
> though

> KELVIN
> Oh mine,

Kelvin shed a tear as he thought to himself what he was missing.

> EMILY
> Hunnn, that's so sweet.

They embraced as they shared a kiss. They both look on at the sleeping babies.

KATY's HOME

Few days later, police were everywhere as they removed the decomposing body from her apartment; the odour was terrible- like perceiving 100 crates of spoiled eggs at the same time. Some forensic team looked around the house for foul play.

KATY'S HOUSE

..Her neighbours were being questioned by the cops outside

                    COP
          You made the call yeah,

                NEIGHBOUR 1
          Yeah, the odour was oozing from
          the apartment this morning

                    `COP
          Yeah, but this morning is the first
          time you perceived the odour

                NEIGHBOUR 2
          I did perceive a little yesterday
          but I thought it probably dead cat
          or something in her apartment

                NEIGHBOUR 1
          Yeah, but could you please tell us
          if it murder or a robbery?

The cop quickly calms the minds

                    COP
          Nah but, we will just wait for an
          autopsy, I think it just a
          peaceful death, she died in her
          sleep. Nothing for you to worry
          about.

                NEIGHBOUR 1

Okay, she did keep to our self a
lot, never really sees her or her
family since she moved in

        NEIGHBOUR 2
Definitely she was an introvert,
saw her only twice

        COP
Oh okay, thank you for your help.
So sorry about the odour, you
probably have to go stay else-
where now.

They all nodded and shook hands; they went on by
their businesses

EMILY'S HOUSE

Mike Came home after his lengthy trip in Chicago- He
branched out to a flower and candy shop and got some
threats for his beautiful wife, he was so happy to be home,
He embraced his beautiful family but there was a sign of
disappointment in the face of his wife, seems her heart
was with kelvin now. The scene dissolved to the bedroom
where Mike tries all his best to please his woman

SEX SCENE!

Emily's face said it all, she was faking it and she was not
really feeling that alpha tributes from her hobby-after
some seconds Mike climaxed in bed and his manhood
went soft afterwards.

        MIKE
       (Panting)
Baby, did you climax

        EMILY

Yes baby, that was great

MIKE
Really, wow, I am, so sorry I left
you all hanging all these weeks. I
made it up this night didn't I? lol

EMILY
Oh yes you did,

They both go on to shower as Emily baths him, Mike
loves to be pampered like a baby ,Emily closes her eyes
and remembers kelvin bathing her the previous night, that
sounds more like it as she nods. Soon after, they head to the
babies room

MIKE
Where the hell is this woman?
Why is she not here at this time?
Has she been behaving like this
since I left?

EMILY
Hmmmm, no I just had to let her
go, she was getting too close to
the kids

MIKE
What did you mean, like sexually close and taking advantage of
them type?

EMILY
I might be crazy but I just have
that feeling, and call it a mother's
intuition.

MIKE
That terrible babe, I am going to
get two nannies now at the same
shift at Night, so they will monitor each other

EMILY
No please I will take care of my babies from now on at night

MIKE
No baby, you stress yourself, I
insist let me-

EMILY
-    no Mike, please, I want my
baby to be close to me

MIKE
That true, alright but if you need
help at any time, we get nannies.

EMILY
Deal and you know we still have
the babysitter in the day shift
which covers for me when I go to
work. So its fine, I am in control.

MIKE
Okay babes, but do you trust the
nanny in day shift, she might be
worse,

EMILY
No way, I trust her, she will
never do that, I tell her

   everything and she does the same
   too, she is really cool

       MIKE
   Okay okay

They go on to play with their kids but mike was unconvinced

EMILY'S HOME

Emily was rushing out to work as she kissed her babies and hubby goodbye, she gave the resuming day shift babysitter some instructions and she rushed off. Mike was busy monitoring the babysitter, his wife's lies about the formal night shift nanny has made him paranoid.
Unaware of Mike presence, the nanny got a little bit upset when one of the twin's vomits on their new cloth she just worn for them

      BABYSITTER
   Really, you just have to spoil
   your cloth after I bath and
   changed your clothes.

...Mike watched and analyzed her reaction critically. He doesn't trust her, he goes on to his car and drove off to a nearby tech shop

CAMERA SHOP

Mike met up with a Nigerian shop keeper at the help desk.

      NIGERIAN MAN
   Hey my friend, welcome

      MIKE
   Hello, please I need help; you see
   my wife told me that she thinks
   our nannies might be sexually

touching our twin babies.

                    NIGERIAN MAN
That terrible, as a father, I
perfectly understand, I watch a
video on YouTube about a nanny
molesting a child for 2 years
and the parents didn't have a clue.

                    MIKE
That terrible

                    NIGERIAN MAN
Yes it is, I commend you for being
vigilant

                    MIKE
You know we can't ever be to
careful

                    NIGERIAN MAN
Absolutely, yes give me one second
let me check some gadget for you sir

The shopkeeper looked around and   then brought a wall
clock

                    CONTD..
Yeah, this looks like an ordinary
wall clock but it has a video and a
microphone in-built in it.

Here, look at the memory card
slot here

                    MIKE
Hmmm, Fantastic stuff, so can it
go all day recording?

NIGERIAN MAN
If you buy 1 terabit gig memory stick, it can go on for 2 weeks nonstop recording. The battery needs replacement every two months though

MIKE
Wow, I will take it.

The two fathers feeling Proud of themselves as they do anything to protect their kids

STATE PRECINCT

In the precinct, different cops doing their thing as they go about the station, the cop that was talking to late Katy's neighbours conversed with his colleague.

COP
Hey Eddie

EDDIE
Yeah, How are you doing?

COP
I got the result of the autopsy of that lady downtown, hmmm

EDDIE
Natural cause yeah

COP
Yeah she died in her sleep.
Are you ready to go?

EDDIE

Sure, you buying the doughnut
today bobby

BOBBY
Yeah yeah.

The two partners go on out of the station to their cop car.

CHICAGO LECTURE THEATRE

Across the city, Mrs. MADISON was giving a lecture in a
1000 seater auditorium which was filled to the bream

MRS MADISON
This is a challenging time for
individuals in the American
penitentiary system,
I wish to be clear with my in-
tention if I become your senator,
the first goal is to review and
change the minimum and maximum prison system, in which we
can help the young inmates. We
will be introducing the training
program called 'Potential entre-
preneurs' across different fields in
the prison system.

The crowd cheered for her as she delivered her power speech

MRS MADISON (CONT'D)
We have potential computer
gurus, artists, engineers, in the
prison system. Via this program we can identify and nur-
ture them to become what they
were designed to become from
heaven, not that bad decision

they have awarded on themselves due to bad choices.

MRS MADISON
They deserve a second chance
at life. We all made mistakes
haven't we?

The crowds shout and echoes "yes" to their speaker

MRS   MADISON
(CONT'D)
you all should come out to vote,
because you are not just voting for
voting sake, you are voting to help
thousands of inmates to turn a
new leaf, you are voting for the fu-
ture of the United States of America, where each and every citi-
zen in penitentiary can become an
asset to the wider environment.
Thank you New York, thank you
America and God bless America
and its citizens.

All crowd cheered....

EMILY'S HOME

In the evening, The couple was playing with their kids in
the sitting room

EMILY
It all boils down to tomorrow now,

MIKE
Yeah months of preparation ends
today, I think mum has a really

good chance to upset Nicolas

EMILY
Yeah, people should be tired of
him, being there for 2 terms now.

MIKE
Yeah, she brings fresh ideas to
the table, after she votes during the election tomorrow, she will leave to Chicago immediately to
our family house there, you know that where we
buried dad, and it was his mission all along to push
mum to be the best of what she can be, and mum
want to be closed to him as they hopefully an-
nounced us the winner.

EMILY
Baby, we should really be with
MUM when they collate and call
the result this election you know

MIKE
Really It has been on my mind all
through the day, but I really don't
know how you would take it

EMILY
She needs us now for emotional
support, but ahhhh, the babies, it
might be dangerous to take them
airborne, you know they are on
medication from runny nose.

MIKE
No No, we shouldn't, please their
health is too important

EMILY

Baby, you go, MUM need you be
her side

MIKE
Baby, I don't deserve you, you
are a rare woman among women,
given the fact I just got back, you
look past that and advise me to
go. I love you baby, I really do.

EMILY
I love you more baby.

They cuddled up as they held onto their babies.

EMILY'S HOME

In the morning, The Nanny was coming to the house as
she resumed her work; Emily went on to bathe while
Mike remembered that he had to place the wall clock in
the kid's room. He zooms off and installs it on the wall of
the kiddie's room.

MIKE
I won't tell Emily, she is too
protective of this Nanny, I hope
she right though,

LATER ON

The couple goes out as they kiss themselves good bye

EMILY
Give MUM a tight hug on behalf of
me, we are winning this for sure

MIKE
Yeah baby

They smiled as Emily drove off to work and Mike's company driver came to pick him up to his mum's residence. Next day, In the series of events, on the news as the senatorial election kicks off between the two mighty contenders. People go about the voting process as Emily, Mike, Mrs. Madison, kelvin all went out to vote. Mike and his mum Jet out to Chicago in time to follow up the election analysis.

EMILY'S HOME

Back to NY, of course Kelvin was there, as Emily grinds on him tirelessly on the couch as they watch the Live polling units' news late in the evening.

THE MOMENT OF TRUTH

Intercut scene between Mrs. Madison's home and Emily's home

TV news reporter and analyst discussed on the TV

TV REPORTED

The last polling unit projection is out. Ladies and gentleman, the incumbent senator won, you can see how close it was, down to the very last polling units. Now we move on to another city's election .....

BACK TO MRS MADISON,

She reacted with great sadness and her child held on to his mama.

BACK TO EMILY

The same sad environment echoed with the adulterous couple

> EMILY
> We lost, we lost

> KELVIN
> Oh shit, I am out of a Job, oh no,
> what the hell am I gonna do
> now

> EMILY
> Baby, you will get another job here

> KELVIN
> This is the perfect job, I head the whole department here, winning this election would have been my short cut to Mrs. Madison I.T security head in her office. I can't go work minimum wage again, no way, I can't!

The heated man rant all over the place, this spook the babies upstairs. The babies cry out like they were competing, they went on to pamper the children.

TWINS ROOM

> KELVIN
> I am sorry babies, daddy didn't
> mean to make y'all cry

> EMILY
> Baby, what do we do now, Mrs. Madison will take over Chicago head office responsibilities, Mike will be here permanently con-

trolling the New York office. Baby
I can't leave without you.

KELVIN
This is bad, I care for you too
baby

EMILY
I cringe when he tries to have sex
with me. I can't continue with
him, he is too boring and weak
in bed. I don't love him anymore.
You made me feel like a woman,
you are the definition of a alpha
male

`KELVIN
Wait a minute,

Kelvin gazed at the babies; he switched his eyes to Emily
and glanced back at the babies.

`EMILY
What is that?

KELVIN
I am about to tell you something,
and I need you to be calm about it
and hear me out

EMILY
Don't dare tell me you're going
back to London.

KELVIN
No, now listen carefully to this,
these babies are ours right? only
ours, not mike

                    EMILY
Yeah?

                    KELVIN
Look at us, don't we look like the
perfect family here, just the four
of us?

                    EMILY
What you getting at kelvin, Mike
is the problem

                    KELVIN
Exactly, what if we remove Mike
out of the equation the same way
we did Katy

                    EMILY
What! Kelvin!

                    KELVIN
Listen hold on,
        (Point at one of the
        twins)

You said he has my eyes, how
long do you think we can keep
this up, what if Mike notices it
and goes on to do paternity test,
you said you don't love him no
more, the only way both of us
can be together with our kids is
through this way

                    EMILY
I don't know, I don't know

                    KELVIN
Hey hey, we can have it all, the

> money, good sex , this mansion,
> our kids, everything, All Mike's
> money surely will go the kids and
> you. Mrs Madison is already old, a
> few years now she will be dead too
> and all the family wealth goes to
> us. We can have it all baby!

She looked really uncomfortable with the idea but she was crazy to believe the idea could work. They successively got the babies to sleep, the alpha male goes on to Emily and concrete his ideas into her and top it up with some good sex she always seem to crave.

SEX SCENE

He pulled the baby cover blinds and went on to sleep with her on the floor right there in the baby's room. Emily kept on biting her lips and she tried all her best to not shout, but this was exactly what she craved, the excitement was orgasmic, as she rolled her eyes up. They go at it through the night.

JFK AIRPORT

Few days later, while in the afternoon, Emily went on to hugged her hobby as he walked through the airport arrivals, the nanny was rolling their babies carts to the husband, passerby were all smiles at their twins looked super-duper cute, what a beautiful interracial family. The scene dissolved into the evening in Emily's home. The nanny finishes her shift, kisses the children goodbye. Emily escorted her downstairs to unlock the security doors and gate, as the nanny leaves, through the gate, kelvin sneaked into the compound. Emily gave him that desperate look as he went on to hide in the building stores. Emily goes in to join her hobby; she then proceeds to the shower. The scene dissolved to their bedroom as Mike and his Wife talk in bed, Mike popped blue pills and he tried to have sex with his wife. she doesn't look too interested unfortunately.

> MIKE
> Come here baby, I know you been
> missing this for a long time

> EMILY
> Nah, I am really tired, it 12:00am
> baby, please let sleep

> MIKE
> I pop two blue pills, I just can't
> sleep,

> EMILY
> No ooo, tomorrow baby

Then they heard cries of their babies again as usually, Emily want to quickly use that as an excuse to leave the hobby,

> MIKE
> No baby, I will go to them, they are crying because
> I am back, they are excited!

> EMILY
> Nah, they always cry at Night, it okay babes,

> MIKE
> Baby, you have been doing the
> baby chores all week long, please
> let me help.

He goes on to take care of the kids in their room, He cares for the babies, making comic facial expressions, then he looked at the corner of the room and remembered he hid a private video camera clock to monitor the ACTIVITIES of the nanny, he goes on to get his laptop in the sitting room, and returned to the babies room.

HE PLAYED THE VIDEO!

He removed the memory card and watched the video playback. He fast forwarded the video a bit as he studied the nanny's action and care but smiled as he knew the Nanny took good care of his babies like they were hers.

THEN, THE SHOCKER!

He saw Kelvin and his own wife coming into the room and taking care of the babies.

Mike's reactions was beyond shocked as he watched the video, his reactions will make the hardest of men almost cry for the poor man has he learnt the truth. He watches on the video

VIDEO PLAYBACK

TWINS ROOM

> KELVIN
> I am sorry babies; daddy didn't mean to make y'all cry

> EMILY
> Baby, what do we do now, Mrs Madison will take over Chicago head office responsibilities, Mike will be here permanently controlling the New York office. Baby I can't leave without you.

> KELVIN
> This is bad, I care for you too baby

> EMILY
> I cringe when he tries to have sex
> with me. I can't continue with
> him, he is too boring and weak
> in bed. I don't love him anymore.
> you made me feel like a woman,
> you are the definition of a alpha
> male

> `KELVIN
> Wait a minute,

BACK TO MIKE

Mike shed tears while looking at the video, he fast forwarded the video as he can't take their dialogue again-**But Mike has missed one very important dialogue in which kelvin told his wife about killing him**

BACK TO THE VIDEO PLAYBACK

The babies have slept off, the alpha male goes on to horny Emily and stripped her cloth off

SEX SCENE

He pulled the baby cover blinds and went on to sleep with her on the floor. Emily kept on biting her lips and she tried all her best not to moan, but this is exactly what she craved, the excitement was orgasmic, as she rolled her eyes up.

BACK TO MIKE

He pumped his fest and grinded his teeth as he watched the sex video. The moaning and grinding of Emily can be audibly heard across the room.

THEN THE MOMENT OF TRUTH!

Emily walked into the kid's room, seeing her husband face and hearing her own voice from the computer. She knew the secret was out now as she stared at the eyes of her husband whose eyes were visibly dilated, as he blinked a million times, his body was shaking like he was having a seizure, he got up walking towards her foaming in the mouth like a K9 beast.

MIKE
You wicked Witch! You being
fucking Kelvin!, Kelvin!, these are his
babies!. You devil, you Bitch! What have I ever
done to you to deserve this!

Emily backtracked as he drew closer to her she ran away from the room. Mike ran after her shouting at her at the top of his voice. Just as Mike ran passed the door frame

SHOCKED!

As the devastated man passed the door frame, Kelvin was already there, hiding outside the door, he grabbed Mike by the neck like a pro wrestler. The clinical serial killer made sure he didn't gave Mike a way out of this wrestling choke to his nose and mouth

EMOTIONAL SCENE

... Emily was frozen looking like a ghost as she watched her husband's eyes, the serial killer still choking him. Mike looked on to her eyes as he stretched his hands towards her, He shed tears as life left him gradually. She closes her eyes crying and leaves Mike to his inevitable death.

> KELVIN
> Listen, it is done, this is not the
> time to be weak, yes crying will
> help at this point, cos you be
> doing that a lot from tomorrow.

Emily was just weak and she followed the lead of the manipulative alpha male. They placed the deceased in his bed and set him up nicely like he was sleeping.

> KELVIN (CONT'D)
> I have to go destroy the evidence,
> listen, you don't have to sleep be-
> side him, tomorrow morning you
> call the ambulance in the morning

> EMILY
> (Crying and sobbing)
> haa oh mine, haa oh mine, What have we done , oh
> my God

> KELVIN
> Control yourself, this is not the place or time to
> lose it. We have rehearsed this   a thousand
> times. you will be okay, just
> stick to the script.

He hugged his girl and went out to destroy the evidence in the kiddies' room.

The scene dissolved into the next morning....

EMILY'S HOME

Ambulance rushed into the compound as the medics went into the house. Emily was crying uncontrollably, as the medics consoled her while they rolled the body into the van. Emily deserved an Emmy for her sad performance. The police came and looked around the place; they took the blue pills for processing. They didn't see anything out of the ordinary.

EMILY'S HOME

Mrs. MADISON was just returning from the mortuary, she was trying to be strong; she just lost a son and an election. The police drove into the compound too,

> POLICE 1
> Mrs. Madison, we are so sorry about your loss

> MRS MADISON
> Thank you

> POLICE 1
> My name is James Waffles, we have tested the blue pills found in Mr Mike's room and we confirm it was indeed save for ingestion, our primary analysis indicated that he might have died from a heart attack caused by injecting two of the power bills, drug overdose is the probable cause. We shall carry out autopsy on him-

> MIKE
> -Please no autopsy, please, officer, this is a terrible time for my family, this is sad enough that my son died from a possible drug overdose of blue pills, the public

will make a mockery of my late
son. Just let him rest in peace,

                    JAMES
          Of course ma'am, we understand,
          once again, we are sorry for your
          loss.

The officers drove off; Mrs. Madison proceeded
into the building. Emily was crying a river with
her friends who were consoling her, Mrs. Madison
fought off tears as she held her daughter in law. It
was such a terrible scene.

BURIAL GROUND

Few days later, Mrs. MADISON, Emily and the rest of the family and friends finish the burial ceremony. Kelvin showed up
too looking all sad, they all head home after the Burial ceremony

EMILY'S HOME

Mrs. Madison walked through the crowd and meet Kelvin,
the expression on kelvin says it all.

                    MRS MADISON
          Kelvin, I like to talk to you in private

                    KELVIN
          Yes ma'am

They head towards the dining area, kelvin looking at her
in suspense

                    MRS MADISON

Kelvin, I really need you to
become the godfather to my
grandchildren. Emily can't do it
alone, I have arranged with the
director of Zimox, you resume as
the lead server security there
next month, please don't turn down
the offer, it's great pay and permanent role too

KELVIN
Oh my god, you are too kind
aunt, I swear to you I will take
care of the kids and be here for
them

MRS MADISON
Thank you dear, I have to get
going now,

Everybody escorted Mrs. Madison to her convoy, she wrapped her hands around Emily as she talked and consoled her, Madam Madison goes on back to the airport to Chicago

EMILY'S HOME

'1 month later' Emily and kelvin arm in arm as they enjoyed themselves with their kids, the love birds seems to have gotten away with Mikc's murder.

SUBURB NEIGHBOURHOOD

In the same city far from the glares and glamour of Emily's estate, to the low income neighborhood but the street looked quite well known- it was where Zack lived, the former boyfriend of late katy.

ZACK'S HOUSE

The girl he cheated with when Katy caught him was still with him.

Both were playing in their bed as his new girlfriend's phone fell into the side bed, as she grabbed her phone, she saw a flash drive there. This was the flash drive stick that flipped out of Katy's bag when he slapped ZACK some months ago.

> ZACK'S GIRLFRIEND
> Hey, guess you been looking for
> this?

> ZACK
> Nah, that not mines

> ZACK'S GIRLFRIEND
> Then who owns it, your other
> flings huh!

> ZACK
> No Patricia, stop that

> PATRICIA
> Yeah, we see about that

She goes on to insert the flash drive into the computer laptop. They saw Emily's files in there, as automatic videos goes on to play the sex tape with Kelvin.

> PATRICIA
> That's your former girl!

> ZACK
> Katy!

HE FLASHES BACK TO THE TIME KATY CAUGHT HIM CHEATING FEW WEEKS AGO

He remembered when Katy visited him for the last time,

ZACK HOUSE- FEW WEEKS AGO

SWINGED THE BATHROOM DOOR!

SHOCKED!

Emily saw her boyfriend, sleeping with his colleague in the shower.

> EMILY
> You bastard, after all i have done
> for you!

> ZACK

> Baby wait it's not what you
> think, it's just sex, I love you
> baby,

She goes on to grab her bag from the bed as nude Zack holds her bag, trying to beg her.

SLAP!

He gave the lover boy a dirty slap, a flash drive inside the bag flipped out and fell into the side bed during the madness. She didn't notice, she grabbed hold of her bags and stormed out.

BACK TO PRESENT MOMENT

> ZACK
> I remember, I think it flipped out
> of her bag when she slapped me,
> that was the night she caught us
> in the shower

> PATRICIA
> She acted classy even though I

was the bitch who knew you both
were in a relationship.

They keep on watching the sex tape of the unknown couple

> PATRICIA (CONT'D)
> She is a freak though, she has
> amateur porn on her flash lol.

TV NEWS

Coincidentally on the TV, it was the 8 o'clock news as they
talked about a company who just elected another CEO after
the death of the former one.

> NEWS ANCHOR
> Good evening ladies and gentlemen, my   name is
> Silver Andrews, and the top news is as
> Follows: Firstly, Zimox has appointed Mr. Douglas
> Walters as the new CEO...

The picture of the new CEO as his name is being refer-
ence

> NEWS   ANCHOR
> (CONT'D) ...After the demise of
> its former CEO Mr. Mike Madison,
> who died of an heart attack, he
> was the husband of the cosmetic
> entrepreneur Emily, owner of
> Glam Cosmetics.

The picture of Mike and his wife as his name was being
referenced was showed on the TV

> NEWS ANCHOR (CONT'D)
> ..Who was also the son of the
> Business mogul Mrs. Tina Madi-
> son, who just contested and lost

the senatorial election a few
months back

Zack watches on the TV as he sees a striking resemblance
of Mike's wife and the lady in the porn video. Zack swings
to his laptop and browses the company Katy was working
formally before her demise, the girlfriend looked over to
what her man was doing on the laptop

> PATRICIA
> Hey, that the same lady

> ZACK
> I know her; she was Katy's boss,
> Katy worked for her!

> PATRICIA
> How the hell did she got the sex
> tape of her boss, was she
> blackmailing her or something?

> ZACK
> Shit, you may be right, Katy be-
> came rich all of a sudden, she
> bought a new car, and I know she
> can't afford that sort of lifestyle
> on her salary.

Then Zack scrolled down another Google article and
saw kelvin's face with Mrs. Madison during the burial
ceremony.

> PATRICIA
> That's the guy on the video!

> ZACK
> Who is he?, he does look alike
> like the late husband

PATRICIA
But much broader

Then, they got his details from the internet and realized who he was, He goes on to check the date the video
was sent to the flash

ZACK
Baby, I can see the guy, his name
is kelvin, gosh this is interesting,
this guy works for the mother in
law of that lady, his the cousin to
the dead guy

PATRICIA
This is crazy, I am confused,
 which dead guy? Mother in law?
 What the fuck you talking about
ZACK
Listen baby, the dead guy, Mike,
that had a heart attack, the
kelvin guy was cheating with his
 cousin's wife, the girl called Emily,
 Wait a minute!

Zack goes back and looked at the Emily pictures with
her kids, he eye lit up

ZACK
Baby, oh mine I think I have add
the puzzles together, what if this
lady called Emily had the twins
for Kelvin during her marriage to
the late husband

PATRICIA
That doesn't make sense, how

would we know that?

ZACK

Katy gave me an assignment to determine the paternity of twins, she provided all the samples for me, I provided her with some tools to retrieve the blood sample without the host knowing. This was her secret mission; she refused to reveal to me, she went crazy after I gave her the results

PATRICIA

Oh mine, Oh God, we have stumbled on some deadly scandal here

ZACK

Yes, Katy was so excited when I gave the result, it must be kelvin who is the real father of the twins, Katy goes on to blackmail them and they killed her, probably after receiving some money from them. Katy took the game too far, she paid with her life

PATRICIA

These people are evil, I hope they didn't kill the husband too, maybe he found out about the affair?

ZACK

Oh shit you are right, I gonna check the cause of both their deaths

They do their research and found out that both

died from their sleep- heart attack!

ZACK

Oh Shit! This can't be a COINCI-DENCE; they used the same technique to kill both of them. they are very clinical leaving no trace back to them.

PATRICIA

Baby, this people might be on to us, what if they know we have this, they might have send their assassins to kill us and make it looks like we died during our sleep too,

ZACK

LET GET OUT OF HERE,

PATRICIA

To where

ZACK

I don't know, police station or something, let just leave here!

The scared couple rushed out towards the downtown precinct.

As montage of events occurred, the couple drew out their stories to the detectives. The story looked ambitious but a fragment of truth seems to be in their story. Soon after, detectives go on to arrest both Emily and Kelvin who were together in her house- but no concrete evidence to link them to both murder, her paternity test was secretly done for their twins, the result was noted by the police.

PRECINCT INTERROGATION ROOM

The detectives' drilled kelvin but his lawyers are there with him

> DETECTIVE JAMES
> You were arrested in your late cousin's house, to top it up you were having an affair with a woman who supposed to be mourning her late husband,

> KELVIN
> I was merely consoling her

> DETECTIVE TAWAD
> We have the sex tape, don't play dumb with us Mr kelvin, you been having an affair with Mrs Emily during and even before she got married. We have all the details here.

> DETECTIVE JAMES
> We know you killed both Katy and Mike, two people who were obstacles to your relationship and the baby you had with Emily

> KELVIN
> What are you talking about, yes I had an affair just once, not illegal, yeah she got pregnant during that unfortunate night with each other, which we both regretted. I didn't kill nobody.

> DETECTIVE TAWAD

You think you are smart?-

KELVIN
-if you had evidence, charge me,
but I guess you got nothing, stop
wasting my time, need to resume
to work!

DETECTIVE JAMES
The only place you going is
maximum penitentiary.

COUNSEL TO KELVIN
We beg to differ, Well gentleman,
since you got nothing, I like to
take my client home

DETECTIVE JAMES
No way, we hold on to him for a
little longer, investigation is
still ongoing.

The detectives leaves the office and proceeded into their
office,

DETECTIVE JAMES (CONT'D)
We have nothing on this guy,

DETECTIVE TAWAD
Katy and Emily's phone record
shows nothing, Emily side of the
story, checks out too, all we have
is speculation, we have no evidence, We losing grip on this two
criminals

                    DETECTIVE JAMES
        Let try out our trick, if it doesn't
        break, we let both of them go

                    DETECTIVE TAWAD
        Our best chance is on the girl,
        Let's press her harder this time.

They busted into the interrogation room like wide dogs,

                    DETECTIVE 1
        Listen Mrs. Emily, Mr. kelvin has
        cut a deal with us and he has re-
        vealed you killed your ex worker
        because she was blackmailing
        you.

Emily's eyes popped up when she thought kelvin had sold
her out, her lawyer was trying her best to keep Emily from
talking as she suspected the trick, but the gullible Emily
was falling for the trick like a rock off a cliff.

                    DETECTIVE JAMES
        He also revealed that you killed
        your husband because one of your
        twins belonged to him. Kelvin
        gets 1 year and you are seeing
        60 to life behind bars with your
        crime.

Emily goes haywire and breaks away from her lawyer's spell

                    EMILY
        Kelvin lied! he was the one that
        killed Katy and my husband,

Emily went on revealing everything as the lawyer looks

her like a complete fool who was spelling the beans faster than a snitch, the detectives recorded everything as they pressed her on the truth. Detective stops the recorder and conversed with Emily

> DETECTIVE JAMES
> You and your man friend almost got away, Kelvin never talked or struck a deal with us, this was our last trick, if you didn't fall for it, you and kelvin would have walked away free. Thank God you did.

Emily looked on in total shock, as her eyes was all glassy, the detectives walked on out of the room as her lawyer looked on at her client in outermost disgust.

PRECINCT

In the Evening, Mrs. Madison was hearing the police recorder as the detectives narrated the story to the crying mother. Another gentleman in white coat walks into the office of DETECTIVE JAMES, The officer conversed with him "Oh yes, Dr. FASAD, welcome, am sure you know Mrs. Madison"

> DR FASAD
> Yes, ma'am I am so sorry about all this, no person deserve to go through this

> MRS MADISON
> (Swollen eyes)
> Thank you, thank you

> DETECTIVE JAMES
> Ma'am, Dr Masad has something

to reveal to you

DR MASAD
Yes, this must come to you in a bit
of a shock to be honest maam, the
twins have different fathers

MRS MADISON
What are you talking about?
Detective, I heard Emily saying
the twins belonged to Kelvin

DETECTIVE JAMES
Yes ma'am but she was wrong

DR MASAD
One of the twin's father is Mr.
Kelvin while the other belongs to
your late son, Mr. Mike

MRS MADISON
What, how the heck is that
possible,

DR MASAD
If two different men mate with a
lady the same day or week, during her heat period, there is 1
in 50 chances that the sperms
of both male could enter her
ovary, thereby she can give birth
to twins of different fathers that
exactly what happened here

MRS MADISON
Oh my God, this too much to handle

DETECTIVE JAMES

You get through this ma'am, God
will help you

DR MASAD
Yes ma'am, please stay strong.

The scene faded into law court in few months later

COURT ROOM

Kelvin and Emily were inside the dock looking all guilty-
the culprit were trying their possible best not to look at
the painful steer of Mrs. Madison toward their direction.
The Judge read out his verdict

JUDGE
Sometimes, I don't believe their
is a devil with a horn, I think
the devils are among us in this
court. I thought have seen
everything in my courtroom but
looking at both of you Mr. kelvin
and Mrs. Emily, you both are among the
worst.

The accused kept looking down as the judge hammered
them with derogatory comments; the Jury had just
reached the verdict as one of the jury slid a piece of paper
to the Judge. The jury found both of them guilty of all
counts labeled against them

JUDGE (CONT'D)
Mrs. Emily you have been sen-
tenced to 30 years as an accomplice in your husband's death and
15 years as a major accomplice
of Katy, you will be eligible for

> parole after 35 years of your sentence, if you are of good behaviour!

She busted into tears as she was screaming uncontrollably, the security shut her up

> EMILY
> My babies, my babies, noh no

> JUDGE
> Mr. Kelvin, you have shown little to no remorse of your callous act, I feel you are not worthy of forgiveness, You are sentenced to 70 years without any possibility of parole for the murder of Miss Katy, you are also to spend the remainder of your natural life in prison without parole for the murder of Mr. Mike.

Kelvin all the while was rolling his tongue in his mouth, the securities removed the culprits out of the court, everyone in the court can't help but feel so sad for Mrs. Madison.

WOMEN PENITENTIARY

Few days later, the scene opened up with Emily being ushered to her prison cell, in there a cell partner was a tall big black tough lady, she conversed to the frightened new comer

> BLACK LADY
> I heard you killed a brother, oh you and I and a lot of sisters here

are going to be talking about that
for a long LONG time.

The black lady cracked a knuckle and other joints,
while looking down at fidgeting Emily like she about
to be fucked up,

> EMILY
> Please I don't want any trouble

> BLACK LADY
> Dear, Trouble is the working cap-
> ital here! Unfortunately for you,
> you pissed off the black com-
> munity here.

They gazed at each other, Emily eyes was all classy now,
the scene switched to another prison

MAXIMUM PENITENTIARY

The non-remorseful kelvin taking a bath and getting
comfortable for a long life in prison, some fellow inmates taking a shower approached him in a friendly
nature,

> INMATE 1
> Hey men, I am Charles

> KELVIN
> Wad up men, am kelvin

> CHARLES
> Cool men; hey meet the rest of the
> crew,

> (POINT TO THE CREW MEMBERS)

Yeah, that Lucas, Morison, Shawn,
Derek, Martins, Atlanta and spooky

> KELVIN
> Nice to meet yall, cool names

The whole crew exchanged pleasantries with the new comer, kelvin thought to himself, *"this is not so bad, my first day I have already made friends"*, as he was shaking all their hands, the last crew member held on to his hand tightly

BASHED!!!!

Charles delivered a thunderous punch to his face; the crew members beat the hell out of the new comer. They conversed with him all bloody up on the floor

> CHARLES
> We know who exactly you are!
> Mrs. Madison refurbished this prison for us and created craft skills platform department which has put hope on inmates including me. With what we make in the departments, 40% of the finance goes to our families out there. Which at least makes us feel like men, oh we will so fuck you up, the devil himself will shed tears for you!

> LUCAS
> You killed our benefactor's child! You destroyed all her will, you caused her unimaginable pain. We are here to repay the favour to you in 10 folds

> CHARLES
> The whole prison crews want to

have a piece of you. We will get the first honours for a month then hand you over to the Clan crew, they are artists you would love their carvings all over your body. Welcome to
hell! The beginning of the rest of your life

The gang goes on their way, kelvin cried for the first time, he cried on the floor feeling remorseful and sense of regret

CEMETERY

Mrs. MADISON with her securities and her nannies go on to the graveyard of his late son. she was trying all her best to be strong but it's not easy, then out of nowhere, a beautiful little girl goes on to give her a red rose

                    LITTLE GIRL
            Don't cry, grandpa said they are
            all smiling to us from heaven. He
            said they are now Angels

                    MRS MADISON
            Thank you dear, yes they are, you
            are so adorable

..as the little lady smiled and talk to her, the
grandpa of the little girl approached from their rear, he
was being escorted by military men to Mrs Madison

                    LITTLE GIRL
            Grandpa, meet my new friend

                    GRANDPA
            Lol, okay Kenya

Kenya goes on to look and play with the twin babies in

the care of the nannies

KENYA
Wow they are so beautiful

Everybody including the securities go on to smile as the little child plays together with them holding their fingers.

GRANDPA

(LOOKS AT MRS MADISON) Hello, I am Air Marshal Jefferson

MRS MADISON
Hello, I am Mrs Madison

JEFFERSON
I know who you are Mrs Madison and am so sorry about your loss

MRS MADISON
Thank you, you   came to pay respect to a loved one yes?

JEFFERSON
Yes, Kenya's mom, father and grandma who was my wife were driving along when a drunk driver hit their car, they all died instantly.

MRS MADISON
Oh my God, I am so sorry, how do you go on

JEFFERSON
I have to be strong for Kenya, she keeps me going and also talking to

her always mask the pain

MRS MADISON
Oh God, life is Brutal; I am in-
spired by your will and courage
Mr Jefferson

Then, little Kenya rushed towards the senior elite
citizens

KENYA
Grandpa, please please let go get
ice cream

JEFFERSON
Sure darling

KENYA
(She holds Mrs Madison
hand)
Please, join us please, they make
great chocolate and vanilla flavor, oh you'd love it

JEFFERSON
Yes please join us, they make
indeed make really nice ice cream, like their Vanilla flavor a lot

The adorable girl eyes was so full of love and Mrs. Madison
smiled back as they both held each other hands

MRS MADISON
OK, darling lol

The beautiful little girl held Mrs. Madison with her left
hand and held her Grandpa with the other hand as they
all walked towards their vehicles. The securities and Nannies in the background were smiling as they followed

them.

....THE
END.......................................

HEARTLESS

(Novel Summary)

In supreme court, FBI filed a fraud case against Harvey(53), a corrupt conglomerate billionaire who is accused of laundering billions for drug cartels via his bank. FBI had planted a mole in his BANK who exposed him. With overwhelming evidence destined to put him behind bars. However, defense Lawyer, Jackson(33) turns the case on its head with incredible tactics. To FBI disappointment, Harvey was found not guilty, but he was fined and stripped of his bank. Harvey's board members are extremely angry at Harvey's corrupt leadership. Opportunistic Vice president Wesley proposes they take a vote of no confidence against Harvey and install him as CEO. Harvey uses dirty strategies to snatch victory from the jaws of defeat during the Board Voting process.

The genius billionaire now thinks himself as Invincible! Harvey soon meets and threatens his DOCTOR, Richard(49). He loaned the doctor enormous cash for his new Hospital. Richard was under immense pressure to get the billionaire a mysterious special package. In another NY Hospital, Dr. John(34), was spending his last days in NY, as he got offered a CMD role in Mandom Community Hosp.(6 hours away from NY) by his mentor Dr. Walters, who was retiring as CMD in MCH. The FBI, still determined to nail Harvey, sent out Special agent Blaze and his 4 man team to stake out Harvey's main casino office. Unaware Harvey's casino building is under watch by the FBI. Robbers hit the casino in a 10 mins strategic sting to avoid NYPD. Blaze seeking excitement, publicity and promotion order his team to jump protocol and storm the casino gun blazing. The AGENTS shows tactical skills in taking out the robbers. However, the lead bugler grabs a hostage. Blaze whispers to his sharpest shooter SAM TO SHOOT THE BUGLER, but Sam objects and hesitates. However, Blaze ORDERS HIM. SAM fires but his bullet hits the hostage's head instead. All the robbers are Killed but Blaze and three hostages are injured. Emotional Sam approaches the Dead hostage. The other AGENTS converge around injured Blaze. Blaze whispers to them 'we will set up SAM and lie that he took that fatal SHOT AGAINST MY ORDERS.

The injured are all treated in the Hospital where Dr. John works. John reunites with his old lost best friend BLAZE from high school. Next day, SAM is betrayed by his TEAM, he was arrested and made the sacrificial lamb to the press. Jocovic an I.T expert working for Harvey discovers and shows shocking video playback of a secret hidden casino camera which videoed Blaze whispering/ordering SAM to take the ill-fated SHOT.

Blaze was lured to Harvey's house where the scandalous video clip was revealed to him. However, Harvey offers him membership to his cult family. Harvey grants Blaze a fortune if he changes loyalty and also if he can get him a SPECIAL PACKAGE.

The rogue agent Pledges loyalty and asks what the package was about?. Harvey reveals his heart was failing, he needs a new heart. Richard has been scouting for new heart illegally for him but has shown incompetent process. Harvey comes up with an audacious plan for Blaze to get him the new heart.

Blaze organises his rogue agents into action, they almost succeeded but encountered unforeseen problems and aborted the plan. Blaze calls JOHN(new CMD/cardiologist in MCH), he casually asks him about ORGAN HARVEST. JOHN reveals he does sabbatical work in Africa and he sees many of such cases. Blaze plans to visit John and ask him to use his connection to harvest a heart for Harvey.

Blaze notified Harvey about JOHN's resume and how the Doctor would do anything for money. Harvey gives an enormous cash contract to Blaze to offer John.

With Harvey's declining health, he discovered RICHARD just exposed his secret to WISELY in exchange for cash and also that Richard has been administering toxic drugs on him in order to cause his heart to completely fail-an attempt by Richard not to pay back a huge debt he owes him. Harvey orchestrated Richard and Wesley accidental deaths before his secret leaks. Harvey and Jackson follow Blaze and his rogue agents to Mandom Community- An attempt to get JOHN to start treatment and detoxify sick Harvey and also find him another heart. Blaze hides Harvey's identity but he discloses other secrets and offers John the CASH CONTRACT. However, John struck Blaze and DECLINED. Harvey was now almost unconscious he promises his two loyal servants half of his fortune if they can just save his life in any cause. Desperate Jackson and Blaze come up with an audacious DAREDEVIL PLAN that shocked the Entire Mandom community.

www.ingramcontent.com/pod-product-compliance
Lightning Source LLC
Chambersburg PA
CBHW052015150726

47999CB00004B/1666